# NOA

# CHILDREN

## OUT OF DISASTER A MYSTERY

# STEPHEN MARTIN

# CONTENTS

# PROLOGUE

I found him in the barn. He seemed okay at first, but he hasn't said a word since I got him into the house. Don't know how long he's been wandering around.

He had this journal on him, some kind of diary. A bit dog-eared and scratchy but, for the most part, legible. Not surprising that he's a bit the worse for wear. If you read it you'll find he's had a rough time.

There aren't any dates in the journal so it's difficult to know how long he's been wandering around; except he refers to last year's evacuation of London. It's not clear when he made the last posting, either.

He talks a lot about two other guys he was travelling with. Don't know where they got to; he was alone when we found him. Anyway, whoever they were, the three of them only seem to have met up after the floods hit.

Funny thing is the writer of the journal doesn't say

much, if anything, about himself. It's like he was watching the others, how they got on and what happened to them, but he wasn't really involved in things. He talks about "I" or "we", when he's remembering something or reporting on the journey, but he doesn't seem to interact with the others. A bit like an author telling a story. Observation and commentary. Maybe he was an author, making notes for a book... but that seems a strange thing to be doing when your world has gone to hell.

Anyway, I thought perhaps you might be able to help us get some answers from him. We need to find out where those others went. We don't want them turning up raiding the stores. Our resources can't support any additions to the group here.

But before you question him maybe you'd better read his narrative; you never know, there may be some clues in there that I missed.

# CHAPTER 1

## THE JOURNAL BEGINS

We stood silhouetted against the dawn light, motionless. Jack had ripped the sleeve from a shirt and tied it round over his mouth and nose.

Ten days on the road and these were the only signs of humanity we had found. The river bulged with its burden, swollen till they were bursting the seams of their garments, hundreds of bodies jammed like lumber against the stone bridge.

"We've got to get out of here," Jack said through the muffle of his shirtsleeve. "Too much death around; don't know how long they've been in the water, but lord knows what diseases they're making between them. We've got to press on."

"Press on? Press on where? We've been travelling for days now and things aren't getting any better. I don't know what you think you're going to find just around the corner, Jack Davies, but it all looks pretty much the same to me: mud and emptiness, that's all."

Josh was near the end of his tether.

"So, you want to stay here, that it? Stay here, and join those poor bastards your stomach swollen like a pig? Well, you can do whatever you want, but I'm leaving. This is the work of those crazy border guards. God knows who or what they think they are protecting these days. Look, look at that one, face half missing. These people weren't the enemy; just came looking for food, the poor sods. They weren't going to find much here but I'm betting it was worse where they came from. So, they get shot for trying to put food in their mouths. Shot by people who haven't recognised that the game has changed. Idiots who haven't figured out there are no good guys and bad guys anymore."

"OK. I'm not the enemy either. We can't stay here that's for sure. I'm for finding a piece of high ground where we can rest up for a while. My toes are skinned from wearing these boots. If you've got a better idea let's hear it. What do you say, Danny?"

Tall, thick set, Danny turned to him with wide eyes. "Thinks? I, er, dunno. These people, what happened? I don't get it, where'd they all come from? Why would anybody shoot them? We got to go, go somewhere else, anywhere else. It ain't safe here."

"Okay. Only question is where to, but we got the message that your vote is for leaving too. Not that you get a vote, nor me. I reckon our self-elected leader Jack here is the only one with a ballot paper."

"I told you, you can do what you like I'm not fussed whether you stay here or make your own way. I wasn't bargaining on having any company."

We picked up our rucksacks from the riverbank.

The morning light was struggling to seep through the grey blotting paper sky. On the opposite bank, lay the detritus of the last storm surge. Uprooted trees lay dismembered, holding beaten supermarket trolleys, plastic bottles, sodden cardboard boxes and a thousand stock items from the local stores, swept down river overnight. Tree branches reached upwards to the clouds in supplication.

"We'll climb that rise to the copse," Jack said. "Maybe we can find some tinder, make a fire and dry off. Still got some beans in the rucksack and those biscuits. We'll decide then where we should head next. Things'll look better with some food inside us."

# CHAPTER 2

## JOSH

Josh understood life on the move. He'd spent five years on the streets of London, homeless. He said that gave him a sixth sense of when it was time to quit a place and where to find safe harbour, for the night. Railway arches and cardboard boxes made his hotel rooms. The martyr's voice in his head kept reminding him that he had chosen this way and deserved no better.

University was supposed to be the place where young people equipped themselves for life. But Josh said it had been a haze of drugs and 'disappointed' tutors. Eighteen months in he had run out of excuses and credits. It was four weeks before he finally summoned the courage to tell his parents that he'd been 'sent down'. Four weeks on a friend's floor, with no reason to get up; four weeks of exhausting the patience of the one friend he had been able to lean on.

When he finally made the phone call 'home' he was numb, past caring.

They say you get the future you create, the one you envision. The only vision Josh had was of the wet winter streets of London pounding pavements endlessly in the early hours, trying to get his head straight. Maybe Josh's indifference and bleak vision of the future had also created his father's terse response on the phone: "Well you'd better find yourself a place and something to do; you need to get a grip of yourself; living with us is not the answer."

That was it. The last time they had spoken. He wondered, sometimes, whether they had ever tried to find him. The martyr in him hoped not, whilst another part of him relished the thought of them scouring the dark alleys and hostels. It would be an education for his father. But he felt guilty about his mother – a woman trapped in a loveless marriage who just wanted life to be safe and 'ordinary'. Josh was her only child and he had turned out to be neither of these things.

Three times, he'd dialled their number in the first year only to put the handset down after the first couple of rings. Soon the impulse faded, the gap too wide, the hurt too deeply lodged. He couldn't put his finger on the time when he stopped thinking about them; they just vanished along with everything else in his history. The only thing that mattered to him by then was the next twenty-four hours: the next place to keep warm, the next fifty pence in the box, the next bite to eat.

The changes passed him by for some months. Yes, he saw the newspaper billboards and heard the chatter of anxious commuters. His box caught fewer coins as the problems got worse. But for a while he could relish the thought of the 'washed classes' having to tighten their belts as food imports became too expensive and then were cut off altogether. There were many more people living on the streets. The police had stopped hassling 'travellers' now they had much worse to cope with.

The power cuts hit just as winter approached. The vents from the underground would stop blasting out warm, stale air and railway concourses and doorways quietly lost their heat.

As the storms became more frequent the arches under Waterloo Station filled with the homeless, huddling around fires made from wind-fallen branches and office waste. The streets had started to fill with uncollected rubbish; strikes and transport interruptions left the City's daily regurgitations of paper piling up on street corners, monuments to the human folly that changed our planet.

Later, some of the street people forced their way into houses and flats left empty by those wealthier souls who had abandoned the inner city for a country retreat. But Josh stayed on the streets.

There had been plenty of speculation in the press about the risks to London but commuters, running on habit, economic necessity and blind disbelief, still packed the tube and rail system until the last few days.

When the storm surge finally came, central London had been evacuated of all but the most stubborn. In their last act the Met Police had emptied the railway arches and Josh Stieglitz found himself walking east along the Mile End Road, out towards the Olympic Park, walking with hundreds of other vagrants and 'guests' of the Salvation Army. He wasn't sure where to head. No one was. There weren't any police visible now. Much of the City's population had already left. Vagrants had started smashing shop windows and looting; some drunk and intent on getting more so. As he got near Mile End tube station, a shaggy-haired urchin of a man bowled over to him waving a whisky bottle like a trophy, saying, "C'mon, pal, have a drink wi' me, where you goin', the party's just startin' round 'ere mate; c'mon, c'mon…"

The stench of stale liquor belched from the man's mouth; a stench that was all too familiar. Josh brushed him aside screaming: 'get off arsehole' and flailing his arms. He quickened his step. Ahead, Stratford. He thought he could catch a mainline train there – if there were still some running. For a few moments he tried to think where he might go. There was nowhere that qualified as home or any direction that had a reason. East made as much sense as anything in this world turned upside down and inside out.

# CHAPTER 3

## DANNY

"You might as well leave school, son. It's not the place for you. Need to earn a living, bring some money in. Anyway, schoolin' and colleges ain't all they're cracked up to be. The students spend their whole time smokin' dope and doin' 'other stuff'."

His father had left; he'd been gone as long as Danny could remember. Mum never mentioned him; she just got on with things. Bringing up Danny and his sister and holding down a job at the local factory were the limits of her horizons.

He couldn't remember much about his Dad. Just a kind of shadow over the house.

Danny struggled at school; couldn't understand a lot of the stuff the teachers talked about. Still, it might have been different if he had found some 'mates'. It can go either way with teenage boys: either they get on your side for some small reason, even the kind of music you like, and then you're OK; or they take against you and then you can't do anything right. It wasn't so much because Danny wasn't smart, it's just that he wasn't 'cool'. He was quiet, didn't have the fast tongue that was essential survival equipment in the schoolyard.

When he came home, upset because of the playground teasing, his Mum would do her best to comfort him: "You may not be the sharpest knife in the box Danny Carson but if the others had brains a tenth the size of your heart, well, they'd…"

She never quite finished the sentence before her tears came again.

So, he left school the day after his sixteenth birthday. A local landscaper took him on, to his Mum's relief. Danny was six-foot three with a powerful frame. The work was hard in all weathers, for a minimum wage, but he loved the outdoors and the quiet solitude of working the earth. No one to call him names there.

He'd been working for five years when the changes, subtle at first, seemed to accelerate. The winters were often milder and wetter than the snowy, frozen-toed landscapes he remembered from his childhood. The sharp, clear skies of those early years were more often replaced by grey, foaming clouds and a gloom that wouldn't lift for weeks on end. The winds would blow with gale force, bending the trees like old men and howling down the chimney in his mother's front room.

Spring seemed at first to start early, then to stop and start as if winter was reluctant to quit. One year the daffodils would trumpet February, the next they would peep out hesitantly in April. They were plagued by ladybirds and mosquitoes from early spring onwards. There had been no winter frost to cull their young. Nature had lost its rhythm.

The river Thames burst its banks downstream and upstream of London a dozen times that autumn. Over three inches or more of rain fell in a twenty-four hour period. Then, with the land waterlogged, the heavens opened again. The new Thames Barrier was about to be severely tested. The rain beating down on the land, ran off into the river system and met the Thames already backing-up due to huge storm surges travelling down the North Sea.

Danny was quiet at home and never said much when there were visitors. He'd stay up in his bedroom, watching TV; not one for going out to the pub or clubs. His Mum worried: "You need to meet a nice girl; how are you goin' to do that stuck up in your bedroom, eh?"

She would ask about his day and get the sparse reply: "The usual stuff."

One day the landscaper telephoned to ask where Danny was. "Why, he's with you isn't he; went out to work this morning?"

"No, he hasn't shown. This disappearing has happened a few times since he started with me. I assumed it was one of those headaches he complains of but thought I'd just check how he is this time. It seems to be getting more frequent. I'll not be able to keep him on if I can't rely on him, you understand."

"Well he's not here; if he's not with you I'm not sure where he is.

Danny came home at the usual time that night. When asked, he just batted off the question saying, "I was working, far as I can say," then went straight off to his bedroom.

His mother checked with Mr Jones each of the next three days, calling him on his mobile to find that Danny was at work 'as usual'.

One day Danny came home and announced that he'd be working in London for a few weeks; would need to travel in early. They were landscaping a garden in a house in Notting Hill. Mr Jones had promised him twice his normal hourly rate to compensate for the travel.

It was in the third day of the job that the evacuation order was issued for London at two p.m. By his usual finishing time of five o'clock Danny was making his way home oblivious to the headlines on the mobile phones of commuters. Reaching Liverpool Street station, the neon display message 'London Evacuation' and the tense voice on the loudspeaker system shook him out of his daydreams. People were running, jumping barriers onto the platforms. Something extraordinary was happening.

He managed to get himself onto the Colchester train but after that things got very confused like a dream, all scrambled up, until he met the others.

*

We reached the edge of the copse half an hour later. A mix of oak, ash and sycamore, the autumn leaves slid underfoot as we looked in vain for tinder. The night's rain had soaked all of the tree fall.

"Unless you've got a blow torch handy, I can't see

us getting any of this stuff to light," Josh said, scornfully. "I don't know what survival book you read Jack Davies, but I learnt a long time ago that you don't squeeze warmth out of wet paper or wood."

"Well maybe you can just shiver yourself dry then," Jack said.

Danny had wandered off fifty yards ahead. Suddenly, he shouted: "Look, over here you two." When we reached him he was pointing to a clearing in the copse. A small, thatched cottage stood there, overgrown but seemingly intact. They waited a few minutes then made their way through the wet ferns cautiously.

Most of the windowpanes were shattered and the paint had long since curled back on the sills to reveal bare, rotting wood. The front door of oak hung off its hinges. Danny put his left shoulder to the edge of the door, lifted it into the vertical and pushed, drawing plaintiff whines from the rusted hinges.

Inside, the gloom was crosshatched by beams of light as the morning sun shot through the broken panes catching dancing motes of dust like a cinema's projector beam.

There was just one large room with a fireplace at the far end and an old pine table and chair in the middle of the floor. To the side of the hearth were bundles of firewood and logs covered in dust.

"No-one around. Looks like the place has been empty for years. But it's dry; the old thatch is still doing its job. Maybe we can get a fire going here."

"You don't think that's an avoidable increase in our carbon footprint then?" Josh quipped.

Soon, the fire cracked and flames licked at the logs. Jack had filled the billycan with some fresh water. It steamed, promising coffee. The biscuits shared out, we sat silently on our haunches each with one hand to the flames to gather the warmth.

The minutes passed. No one spoke. What was there to say? What is there to talk about when the world has suddenly emptied and all the things men took seriously seem to have come to an end? What do people talk about most of the time? Things like what they're planning to do at the weekend; where they're going to go on holiday. About the future: plans and hopes. But when all the futures people expected get washed away, what takes their place then? What do you talk about then?

And talking about the past doesn't seem right either. It's like the past has suddenly become a bastard and doesn't belong. Better to just forget. So all you're left with is 'now': a little bubble of time filled with what *is,* with no space for what was or what may be.

It was Danny who eventually broke the silence.

"I don't know where Mum and my sis' have ended up. I knows they are out there somewhere. We're country folk; they knows how to look after themselves. It was so dark, all the lights out when the water hit. I just got carried away by it. Hope they was at home and could shelter upstairs.

"I got to get back there and find them."

"Most of the county is likely to be under water. How are you going to get around? The rain last night would have just made it worse." Jack's realism overlooked compassion.

"They're dead."

"What?"

"They're dead," Josh said more firmly.

"How do you know? How do you know what happened?"

"Stands to reason. If that floodtide travelled up the Thames and hit London so hard what's it likely to have done to Essex villages? They're gone and you holding on to hope isn't going to bring them back; it's just going to make you do something stupid. You go back there and you'll die too. There's no way to get around, no fresh water or food and there's going to be disease as soon as that hot sun breaks through the cloud cover."

"How come you know so much? I can't just…"

"I'm telling you it doesn't lead anywhere. You're bound to feel like this but it doesn't lead anywhere. You've got to look after yourself Danny; the others are gone. You're on your own now."

Danny's head slumped towards his chest and his eyes stared at the base of the fire.

Alone. Well, what's so different? He'd mostly been alone through his life, hadn't he? But this would be a different kind of alone. Before, he was alone in crowds, alone in that schoolyard. Would this be more, or less than that kind of alone?

"They'll be okay. I knows it. We'll meet up. The water'll go down eventually. Probably sat around a fire somewhere just like us."

"Whatever," Josh said. What was the point of rubbing the poor, dumb lad's nose in it anyway? Who was he to insist on reason? Maybe it was easier for him to give up hope; he'd had some practice at that.

The smoke spiralled up to the rafters. One of the

logs sighed and slumped, breaking where the yellow embers had weakened it. Jack threw on another.

The sun's rays strengthened through the windows throwing spotlights onto the floor like a stage set. Huddled figures sat, clothes steaming, in the only warm, dry place left in an indifferent universe.

Some time later Danny muttered: "No job, now, either."

"What?"

"No job, I says. I don't have no job any more. Can't landscape in a flood, can you?"

"I wouldn't worry about it. I haven't had a job for years. Hasn't held me back has it?" Josh said. "Look at us: a university drop-out, a banker and a gardener. We're all in the same boat now, aren't we? Or the same ark, maybe, huh?"

Jack had noticed a long mirror hanging from one wall. The glass was covered in dust. He gathered the end of his jacket sleeve and rubbed away at the grime, then stood back.

He caught his breath at the apparition that greeted him. The retreat from the City had left no time for a change of clothes. He was still in his regulation City pinstripe. But now the jacket and trousers looked like something you'd see on a circus clown; arms and legs shrunk and the fine English worsted crumpled and stained.

His shirt looked as though it had seen a hundred boozy nights and sleepovers without a change. Around his neck with its knot drooping at half-mast was a Liberty tie. For a moment his hands reached up in habit as if to tighten and straighten it then fell limp by his side heavy with futility.

His face was covered with a greying beard.

Maybe there wasn't much difference between him and Josh after all. Half drowning followed by weeks, or was it months, on the road left him doing a passable impersonation of a tramp.

Danny gave Josh a dumb look then carried on.

"All them flower beds I planted round at Mr and Missus Richardson's; and that rockery at… All under water. And my mower…"

"I don't believe it. You go from worrying about what happened to your family to worrying about your flowerbeds. What is it with you? Your sense of priorities is a bit bent out of shape if you ask me; warped by being in that river too long would be my guess; some of the water got into your brain, assuming there is any grey matter up there that is…"

"Leave the boy alone! He's confused that's all. Just leave him be," Jack Davies growled.

"Since when did you become the protector of the weak?"

"I ain't weak 'n if you ain't careful you'll feel how strong I am. Your college learning might have given you a sharp tongue and I knows I can't win that fight but if you want to feel the back o' my dumb hand you is goin' about it the right way." Danny felt a rising in his chest like the one he'd felt so many times in the schoolyard.

"Alright, alright. No need to get physical. Sure sign of the breakdown of human society."

"That's rich coming from you," Jack said.

Josh retreated into sullen silence.

A few hours later, we were on the move again. What few rations we had managed to gather from the pantry of a deserted house five miles back had now been reduced to half a packet of digestive biscuits. At least the rucksacks were light. A billycan, two knives, matches, a sleeping roll each and sundry items of clothing scavenged at the house was all we carried.

The unspoken certainty between us was that, without fresh water soon, we would be added to the statistics, assuming someone was still keeping tally.

Danny broke the silence: "They're bound to send out some teams to rescue people some time soon. They're just not goin' to let people sink or swim. They'll use the army to get supplies out to people."

"Who are *they*?" Josh responded. "Are *they* the self-sacrificing, brave politicians, we, you, voted into power? The ones who did such a good job ensuring food was cheap and plentiful when we had working trains and boats and planes and a road transport system? Are those the ones you're talking about? The same people who made such a good fist of keeping the peace that our prisons were full and whose energy policy made us hostage to oil rich states whilst changing the seasons. These are people we can rely on, for sure. In fact why don't we just sit down here and wait for them to come along with a three-course dinner and wine. I'm sure we are bound to be top of their list of priorities."

For minutes, the only sound was the scrape and crunch of gravel as weary feet trudged that railway track the sleepers just too widely spaced for a tired man's stride.

Jack said, "We can argue where blame lies as much as you like but unless we find fresh water and food soon then all bets are off. And sure as hell there are going to be others looking for the same things. I doubt that anybody has got much of a plan right now but to scavenge for enough to keep body and soul together. We'd better be ready to fight to stay alive. Nobody's going to be the least bit interested in political or social debate in this mess."

# CHAPTER 4

# JACK

Jack Davies was a corporate survivor. An investment banker with twenty-five years' experience learns where the landmines are in the corridors of New York and the City of London and how to dodge them on the way to the top.

He said that he joined directly from school with 'A' levels, one of the last generations to start at the trading desks at the age of eighteen.

Within two years they gave him a management job in charge of the European Commercial paper desk and from there he started his headlong rush to become the youngest CEO in the history of Rothsberg. A rush that barged through all obstacles, mostly human, on its way.

With successive promotions came marriage to the

daughter of one of the City's doyens along with progressively larger houses, in city, country and beachfront with enough cars to fill the garages at all of them. But no children came.

"Not bad for the son of a bricklayer," he would remind dinner party guests.

Jack's trademarks now were a shock of greying hair, red braces and monogrammed cufflinks – the essential plumage of the investment banker. But it hadn't always been that way. Somewhere in Knightsbridge, in an old shoebox full of family monochrome, was the boy in short trousers, hand me down shirt and scuffed shoes. Jack found that humble beginnings, grammar school and a Yorkshire accent were all badges of honour in the new City, Americanised and tolerant of the working class aspirant in a way the previous old-school-tie generation had not been.

Money was the new breeding, Jack would say. It was the protective overcoat too when cold winds blew. Jack had ridden out two recessions by 'going into cash' at the right time and ensuring anyone who might have presented competition at work was shunted off into some siding where they were bound to fall to rust before finally exiting with a generous severance package.

Of course he'd learnt about 'leadership'. He submitted to the annual 'off-sites' of the top management group, building things with plastics straws, 'cancelling' the enemy with paint balls and burying them later in the bar till the early hours. Jack was always there at the death. 'If you go to bed last, they can't plot against you' was the unspoken axiom.

The women in his life came and went, but his wife of twenty-two years standing, stayed; and it seems she stayed quiet about Jack's extra-curricular habits. Once you give a thing a voice it's not easy to buy its silence again. And each of them needed the social 'norm' that marriage conferred without wanting to go looking again. So the two of them colluded to keep the silence.

Jack could see that the credit crisis was just the start of things unravelling. But he'd called it wrong: "Just a temporary correction, a hangover after a wild party; we all wake up, take a dose of salts and within a few quarters of bumpiness we get back to work, riding the next wave." The bumblebee inside the jar can see the big wide world outside but doesn't know he's trapped and that the air will run out soon.

Government intervention overshot and inflation took a grip; that spectre that central bankers worry about on our collective behalf. It pushed through the surface like a spring shoot, then accelerated skywards. The oil producers were not of a mind to do the Western economies a favour; China, India and Brazil were sucking in natural resources to feed their turn at industrial and commercial revolution; commodity prices and distribution costs went exponential. In parallel, the Earth reached another tipping point: population growth and expectations of a new burgeoning global middle class allied to institutionalised waste in the West meant that Mother Earth, however sexed up with hormones and fertilisers, could not keep pace with mankind's appetite.

Food exporting nations slammed on the brakes, prices sky-rocketed, politicians were sacked to no avail as the laws of supply and demand interacted with geo-politics to change comfortable English lives forever and to start nations marching beyond their boundaries in search of life-sustaining resources.

In the first year of this dialectic, the commodities trading desk had a record year and so did Jack Davies' bonus pot.

From there on it was downhill. As international trade flows started to dry up, so international finance flows started to freeze. Banks and financial institutions again changed their view of risk and pulled in their horns as regulators brought the bonus culture to its knees. Stagflation followed in Western economies and Governments shorn of tax receipts cut back dramatically on infrastructure investment.

Josh would say that the ground was prepared for man's short-sightedness to unleash the fury of nature.

We all remember day after day of images of overseas disasters crowding the TV screens and front pages. Cyclone in Burma; hurricanes out of season along the east coast of the US; millions homeless in Bangladesh; drought in Australia; failed harvest in Canada; extreme heat in North Africa. Most were far enough away to draw sympathy but not fear. Until the riots in Madrid and Rome. They had started as people took to streets to cool off in water from the standpipes but escalated as the temperatures rose. The first food shortages in stores had been met with a short-lived stoicism, with people holding onto the belief that normal service would soon be resumed. But as the shelves grew emptier, accelerated by panic buying, the public mood changed and the dogs of chaos strained at the leash.

Police shootings of civilians in the major cities of Western Europe brought the hunger of Africa into the front parlour of the developed world. CNN filled the world's eyes with images of forest fires raging in record temperatures across North America. The US closed its borders to civilian traffic, but it could not stop the flow from Mexico even with a hail of bullets.

The world's politicians gave their assurances and commitment to work together to meet the 'greatest challenge facing mankind'. A cynical population knew then in its heart that the game was almost up.

The British Prime Minister 'refused to be drawn' on the nature of contingency plans. An impatient public deduced there were none.

The government announced there could be no restoration of the sea defences around the Wash and Norfolk coast. It was 'unaffordable in today's economic conditions and we have to be realistic about sustainable defence against the rising levels of the world's oceans and seas'. The ice sheet covering Greenland had retreated by 30% within the space of three years. Scientists reported that the changes were accelerating.

Vast swathes of Cambridgeshire and the Fens were abandoned to the rising level of the North Sea. Several million hectares of arable farmland would be submerged.

The power cuts increased as ageing generating stations misbehaved. Water supplies suffered as pumping stations stopped their life-giving work.

Then, in the final throes of a helpless Government, the BBC reported it was operating under undisclosed limitations on the news it could report. Limitations imposed by the government 'in the public interest'.

Many had hoped for a quiet deceit, an invisible withholding of the truth, a make-believe that they could all row along with.

Just a few weeks later the evacuation of London was underway.

Jack told us he had made plans for such an event. He had access to the newsfeeds throughout the working day. As soon as it became odds on a general evacuation order would be made his driver was to be outside the Bank's doors in Canary Wharf.

His mate Richard had a weekend estate in Suffolk. He had stockpiled provisions. That would be their bolthole until some order was restored. Of course no one believed it would happen; stocking up the barn was just a bit of fun, a make-believe, reminiscent of younger days in South Yorkshire lying on his belly in the farmers field eating peas and getting stomach ache; of afternoons raiding old man Johnson's orchard and gorging on unripe pears as hard as wood.

When the time, came Jack's attention was on the gyrations of the markets. The Hang Seng had closed off 35% overnight; the Chicago futures exchange was suspended and London was a sea of red. Jack was in damage limitation mode trying to liquidate his positions. When the feed signalled: 'London evacuation to begin' it was already too late. The streets were a parking lot as Porsche engines growled and horns signalled the rising panic of a whole industry trying to save its skin. His driver was nowhere to be seen. After half an hour of chain-smoking outside the tower, he decided to head for the DLR. He decided he'd make for Stratford and pick up the eastbound train there. Richard could pick him up from Colchester or Ipswich. It was time to get out.

When he reached Stratford, the platforms were heaving with startled people. Cancellation notices screamed from the electronic destination boards. Overcoated City workers leant over the platform edge desperately willing a train to appear.

Six fifteen. The October night was closing in. Suddenly he heard the telltale buzzing of the overhead wires. Wherever this one was going he had to get on. As the train's brakes screamed, he pushed his way towards the edge of the platform.

A short squat man to his left pushed back hard with his shoulder into his ribs. "Hold on mate, wait your turn."

The train slowed like an expiring breath. Jack Davies pushed forward further; moments passed. He could see bodies pushed up hard against the doors.

Finally, the doors ground open and grim-faced commuters bulged out on to the platform. Some got off, following a Pavlovian habit to make their last connection.

He saw a gap and launched himself past the last line of people, into the space.

The squat man shouted and waved his fist in the air, "asshole, there's plenty of people here before you, get off you bastard". He was pushing to get to the door but the rank in front of him closed up. Two tall, thickset guys turned and started arguing with him.

Jack Davies looked down at his feet trying to ignore the fracas on the platform and the stares around him.

Moments later the doors started to close, stopped then re-opened. "Please do not block the doors. Repeat, please do not block the doors."

The three men on the platform were struggling with each other now. One of the tall guys had gripped hold of the squat man's overcoat lapel and was pushing him back.

Again, the doors started to close. Jack Davies pulled in the trailing hem of his great coat and finally the doors snapped shut. The engine gave a tug and the crowd on the platform moved past the windows like the slowed up frames of a movie reel gradually gathering pace.

Jack looked firmly at his feet, at once relieved and ashamed.

In the same carriage, Josh Stieglitz hung onto the strap dangling from the roof, thankful that the station ticket barrier attendants had long left their posts.

"This train will terminate at Colchester," the driver's voice boomed out over the intercom.

# CHAPTER 5

## EMPTY WORLD

Below, the floodwaters still raged.

"We'd better keep to high ground as much as we can. There's no telling when we'll get the next surge," Jack said, trying to impose some limited authority over events.

The other two were licking their wounds and fell into line silently.

We stopped and looked around us. As far as the eye could see, the undulating plains either side of the Thames Estuary had been flattened by the mud-brown floodwaters. The dark furrowed earth made ready for winter was now four or five feet below the surface, its sharp folds blunted by the flood. The hedgerows and their inhabitants lay suffocated; the earths of foxes and badgers dens water-filled like a sponge. And now the silence – the silence which comes when all the chatter of the world is stilled under a liquid blanket. The silence when the rustle, bustle of worms and insects in the litter of leaf fall is drowned; when the hedges and trees are robbed of air and the birds that nested in their branches now become homeless; when men's hubbub is laid to rest and the volume is turned down on all the busy backcloth to life.

To the east was a railway embankment struggling to stay above the surface of the waters. We headed down towards it. That would lead somewhere; and somewhere was where we needed to go. Somewhere we could find something remaindered from this apocalypse. A place with clean water, food and a place to sleep in the day. Somewhere that had the basic things of life that Jack Davies had never before had to go looking for.

For hours we followed the tracks. In places the gravel bed supporting the line had been partly washed away. We hopscotched gingerly along the exposed sleepers hovering above the brown silted waters.

"This must be the mainline out of Liverpool Street. By my reckoning we must be around twenty miles out of London. We ought to hit Chelmsford soon. Maybe we'll find something there."

"Maybe," offered Josh.

The sun had broken through the cloud cover now and was beating down on our heads. Jack tore another strip from one of the shirts in his rucksack and bent down to wet it. Suddenly the sleeper shifted under his foot, his left ankle skidded underneath him and he pitched sideways over the rail, down into the muddy waters.

The girth built over years of business lunches and dinners hit the surface with an almighty splash and then disappeared from view. Seconds later he bobbed up, back arched, arms and legs flailing only to collapse back under the surface.

"Jack!"

A moment later two arms reached up and beat the water; Jack's head surfaced again his eyes staring heavenwards.

"Christ. The guy can't…"

Another great splash. Danny had jumped in and in a flash was behind Jack, right arm under his armpits and left arm rowing to manoeuvre them back to the track. Danny's big hands scooped the foaming water like a bucket.

"Grab him. Pull!"

Josh braced himself against the rail and pulled with all the strength he could summon. Slowly the limp frame slid up onto the sleepers and rolled onto his side.

For a moment all was silent.

Then, as if a key had been turned in the ignition, Jack Davies' body convulsed and vomited a stream of water, chest heaving and gasping for air.

It was half an hour before he was ready to start walking again.

None of us said anything: least of all Jack who seemed more embarrassed than grateful that Danny had saved his skin.

\*

"Look. On the horizon, there's something. What is it? Can't make it out." Josh held the flat of his hand above his eyes to shield out the sun.

"Don't see nothin'," Danny said.

"Look. It's moving," Josh insisted.

Danny screwed up his eyes and waited, stock-still.

"Yeah, I see it. What… ?"

"It's a man, a boat; both. He's heading this way. Wave, come on flap your arms, he can't miss us. We must stick out like a sore thumb on this embankment. First sign of life we've seen. So we're not alone in this mess."

A slim figure was silhouetted against the glare bouncing off the surface; beneath it was a long shape lying low in the water.

"It's a punt or something like. See the long pole in his hand. He can reach the bottom, over there at least."

"Hey! Over here."

"He's heading our way."

Minutes passed as Josh and Danny continued to wave and shout.

Jack Davies had crouched down on the track, waiting but not contributing to the others' SOS signals.

The boat kept coming towards us. A quarter of a mile away now, perhaps less, but with no sign of recognition from its pilot.

The boatman's hands climbed slowly along the length of the pole then, with a final shove, gathered it in again. Then he stopped. The figure stiffened, trailing the pole in the water, head turned in our direction.

"He must see us now, must be able to hear us," Josh shouted.

As soon as the words were out, the figure on the

boat swung the pole out wide and turned the bow; away. The boat swung round till its owner's back was towards us. He planted the pole, gave a full-shouldered heave and set the craft on a new course.

"Hey. Where you going? Over here!"

"He's leavin'. Do you think he saw us?" asked Danny.

"Sure, he did. How could he not? We're the only things sticking up out of the water for miles except a few treetops. How many trees do you know wave their limbs and make a racket, like we were making? He's just buggered off, selfish bastard," Josh said.

"Why?" Danny looked down at Jack.

"Scared. You spot a bunch of strangers near the end of the world as we know it and maybe you'd be scared. He's got his boat and I'm guessing food and water. He's hanging onto what he's got. It's survival of the fittest time."

Nobody said a word for the next few miles. Sometimes reality takes a while to sink in.

Jack thought about the world he'd abandoned. The markets would be suspended. Electricity supplies out and the dealers scattered in the evacuation. For a fleeting moment he thought of the short position on

Eurobonds he'd meant to close out on Monday morning. Old habits die-hard. Then the futility hit him, laughed at him.

He imagined the dealing rooms deserted, silent; the drowned corpse of capitalism struck dumb by Mother Nature's irresistible forces.

The exchanges systems were run from a site out of town with a separate contingency site for back up in the event of some disaster. But had they planned for something like this? If the sites were ok then the trading systems could be run, but the dealers would need secure access PCs to trade and with whom? Nobody was going to buy a coffee bean, still less a bond, derivative or share if they couldn't trust that there'd be a market the next day. You can't eat digital share certificates or even paper ones come to that.

But if the markets have been down for days what about the banking system? The 2007/8 credit crunch would look like a mild bout of constipation by comparison.

Somewhere, recorded in binary form on storage disks, was the sum total of the wealth he had worked twenty-four by seven for thirty years to accumulate. But the institutions and systems needed to turn those bits and bytes into food, heat, light, and power were in disarray. And it wasn't clear whether all the kings men could put those pieces back together again.

Jack looked into the distance. Water everywhere. He needed a whisky. This had to be some sort of nightmare, a virtual reality ride. Disasters like this get talked about by scientists, debated by politicians, they're the stuff of movies, but they don't happen for real. If they happen at all, they happen sometime far in the future to people he's never met and doesn't care tuppence for. Most of all, things like this don't happen to a Master of the Universe. The real world is bid offer spreads, futures contracts, forex options, isn't it? These are the flora and fauna of the world of the markets; the world of money which makes the so-called 'real' world go around. The markets which pay school fees, put roofs over people's heads, pay for holidays, fuel our cars, heat our hot tubs, make and ship silk shirts, high-definition TVs and all the other 'essentials' of modern lives. The markets don't flood. They rise and they fall; they make rich men and bankrupts; they frustrate Governments; they invest, they divest but they don't flood for Christ's sake.

But here he was. one of the biggest players in the City of London with a net worth of over £200m, walking along a railway track in some other lost soul's boots; walking a track with a dropout and a gardener with 'learning difficulties'. If reality is defined as something that exists and does its own thing, including stubbornly persisting independent of the observer, then this was reality. He'd even tried pinching his thigh and blinking fast to see if he could dislodge a piece of this new reality, make a crack in its façade.

The other world was gone. He faced a different kind of fight for survival; one where his 'old world' skills had no relevance. Yet somehow Jack felt calm; calm even though his world had just been rubbed out. He had been lonelier, more on the edge than this at least once in his life. Watching markets start to rise when you're sitting on a billion dollars' worth of short positions can be life threatening if you measure life in old world terms. It can be deeply lonely to know you face the loss of everything you hold dear. A loss that is public and not shared, brings shame; it singles you out as a 'loser', someone to be avoided. It's a fall made steeper by other people's success; like being expelled from the Promised Land.

He was finally 'saved' by the misery of others. Terrorist strikes reversed market sentiment enabling him to get out with a bloody nose.

But even that shouted his aloneness, his

separateness. When your survival makes you hope for disaster; hope for something that costs so much misery for others then you know you are living in a different world to most of the human race.

His mouth dried with the aftertaste of that shame.

We passed scattered farmhouses and hamlets without signs of life. The carcasses of sheep and cows occasionally bobbed into sight swollen drum tight by the water and what looked like weeks of decay. It was late afternoon. The air was thick with flies hovering wherever we spotted dead livestock.

"This isn't looking like a winning idea," Josh said with a strong accent of blame.

"I didn't hear you come up with a better one," Jack retorted.

"No need to be so touchy, I'm just saying…"

"Look. I'm not interested. You want to do something different be my guest."

"It's your way or nothing, right?"

"If you like. Or even if you don't like. I'm not telling you what to do. You're your own man, can make your own decisions."

"You're the one who said we should stick together."

"Well, let's just say that policy is up for review. All I hear from you are moans. No wonder you were on the streets. Attitude problem."

"It's none of your business why I was on the streets and I wouldn't expect the likes of you to have the faintest understanding…"

"The likes of me?"

"Yeah. 'Buddies' we called you… as in 'buddy can you spare a dime'. Throwing a few pence in a box to salve your consciences whilst you commute back to your oh so comfortable suburban, detached lives. Well, look at the mess that's got us into."

"Oh, I get it. The guys who pay the taxes are the villains. Time you grew up. That chip on your shoulder belongs to some Che Guevara worshipping, stoned out of his mind, adolescent student."

"I don't know why you two argue so much." Danny tried to get into the role of peacemaker.

"Well, I do. We're chalk and cheese, that's why. Two ends of an economic and social spectrum. Have's versus have not's. Solzhenitsyn's warm guy who can never understand a guy who's cold. He's a warm 'have' and I'm a cold 'have not'. Egyptian linen sheets versus cardboard boxes. Oh, just one more difference, him and his consumer buddies have warmed up this world big time. The likes of me just breathes $CO_2$ out; he vomits it with his four litre engines, mansions in town and city, flights…"

"You're out of date mate. I left the Porsche back at the office and in case you hadn't noticed we're walking the same track so get off your fucking high horse," Jack sneered.

It was then that Danny shouted: "Look! Over there. Buildings. A town." Colchester was an island rising gently above the floodwaters like some poor man's Camelot.

The railway embankment took us in the direction of the town centre past overgrown suburban gardens. A thick blanket of silence lay over the broken-paned, sentinel houses edging the railway line.

"Empty? Where is everyone?" Danny gave voice to the question hanging in the air. "Why would they have left?"

"Maybe they weren't sure how high the flood waters would reach," Josh said.

"Spooky."

We stood facing a large, detached house and its back garden. The lawn was overgrown with nettles and long grasses a foot tall and gone to seed. A swing creaked in the breeze. On the left border was a row of fruit trees, at our feet the blackened remains of their rotting autumn throws.

"No-one's touched this garden for months, maybe a year," Danny whispered.

We scrambled down the side of the embankment and Jack swung open a gate to enter the garden.

"The back door's open. Shall we have a look inside?"

"What if there's somebody…"

"You joking? C'mon the place's deserted, can't you see?"

"Well, I just… It don't seem right just bargin' into somebody's place like that," Danny said.

"There's nobody about, but we'll knock on the door if you like," Jack said.

He rapped firmly on the door, "Hello, hello, anyone there?"

We strained our ears. A muted scuffling sound came from inside.

"Hello. Anybody there? We're just looking to re-fill our water cans; don't be alarmed." Jack wasn't sure why he added the reassurance; it just seemed like a place and time where you needed to say that kind of thing.

He pushed the door gently open. "Hello? Anyone there?"

A few moments passed as our eyes adjusted to the gloom. Josh felt for a light switch either side of the door, more out of habit than expectation. His fingers found the smooth plastic and flicked it down. Nothing, of course.

"Phew," Danny screwed up his face and put a hand to his mouth and nose. The air was fetid. We were in the kitchen. In the centre of the room was a long oak table, with the remains of a half-eaten meal now covered in mould. To the left a large refrigerator door hung half open. At one end an Aga oven with clothes draped over the bar along its front.

The scuttling was coming from a corner near the sink units. "Rats," Josh said.

Josh tried the fridge. Rancid butter; a half bottle of yellowing, coagulated milk, which had separated out; a pile of rotted fruit.

"Hello," Josh shouted from the bottom of the stairs.

"Forget it," Jack said, "there's no one here. Hasn't been anyone here for quite some time."

Jack tried the cold water tap. A stream of brown,

brackish water flowed out limply.

"Water supply's contaminated, by the flooding I guess."

"Can we boil it?" asked Danny.

"Maybe. See what you can find in the cupboards, any plastic bottles. We'll fill a couple in case we can't find anything better."

"Let's get out of here, it's creepy, and I'm not keen on being anywhere near those rats," Josh said heading out of the back door.

Jack filled two plastic, litre bottles that Danny found in the cupboards above the refrigerator, gave one to Danny and put the other in his rucksack. "Maybe these houses on the outskirts were abandoned because they were too near the flood plain of the river. It's possible everybody got moved to higher ground nearer the city centre."

None of us had much confidence in the hypothesis, but we re-joined the embankment and headed further into town.

For a mile or so the track hugged the boundary of row upon row of terraced houses, all silent, looking through dusty, cracked windowpanes with vacant stares.

"Listen," ordered Jack.

In the distance, a solitary dog barking. "Well, the dogs are living on something," Jack said.

Half a mile further, above the rooftops, stood the big red 'M' sign.

"Let's get off the track and see what's over there," Jack said. "Could be a retail park, shops."

We walked along a narrow tarmac road separating two rows of terrace houses. The dogs barking was getting louder.

Here and there were cars stood at odd angles to the pavement, mottled with bird droppings, windscreen and windows blurred by dust and rain streaks.

"Wherever all these folks have gone, it looks like some of them went on foot. Why would they do that?" Jack said, not expecting any reply.

"Fuel stock-outs. They probably hadn't stock-piled supplies. Remember those fires and explosions when people started hoarding the stuff. I reckon it was worse than we were told. I reckon a lot of things were worse than we were told," Josh said.

We rounded the corner and across a dual carriageway saw the signs of the shopping centre. It was dusk but the neon signs were lifeless. The car park was scattered with supermarket trolleys like the skeletons of some long extinct species. A breeze had gathered during the late afternoon and was now playing, kitten-like, with the cardboard boxes on the forecourt of Morrison's supermarket.

To the left the Electrical Discount warehouse sat silent, disbelieving as if expecting someone suddenly to blow a whistle and reinstate the throngs of acquisitive shoppers and commission hungry sales staff. 'Prices Slashed' posters shouted out in obese, red and white letters as if designed for the short-sighted and hard of hearing, shouting like a drowning man a mile out to sea off an empty beach.

Josh felt a sickly ache in the pit of his stomach. Was it hunger or something else?

"Takings must be down this week," he quipped nervously to fill the void for a moment.

"We might find some canned food and water in the supermarket," Jack said.

The electric doors were shut but Danny's strong fingers prised a gap and they gradually opened wide enough to enter sideways on.

The shelves cut the gloom like the hulks of shipwrecks peering out of a sea mist. On the floor of the aisles, packets of washing powder, muesli, cornflakes and rice had burst, their contents weeping onto the floor. Each time we rounded the end of a run of shelves we heard the tell-tale scuttling of rats.

"We can forget the dry goods; I doubt they'll be edible and the rats have probably got at most of the stuff. Head for the cans — soup, vegetables, juices, fruits and the like. I'll look for the bottled water."

Josh took charge of one of the trolleys abandoned in the aisles: "Look for the special offers Danny."

Half an hour later, the trolley full of assorted cans which passed the sell-by date test, Josh and Danny stood at the checkouts. Jack was wheeling in our direction from the drinks section.

"So what happens next?" asked Josh. "Where the hell are we going to take this stuff; I've left the 4 x 4 at home and the buses aren't running. Should we call a cab?"

"Very funny," grinned an oddly relaxed Jack Davies, his cosmetically whitened teeth beaming in the gloom.

"What have you got there?" asked Danny.

"Water. Litre bottles. Should last as a while."

"And in your hand?"

Jack lifted a bottle to his lips.

"Is that whisky?"

"Sure is," said a mellowing ex-banker. "Want some?"

"No, I don't drink," Josh said.

"What, worried about a hangover, work tomorrow?"

"I just don't drink… that's all."

\*

We decided to stay in the supermarket for the night. A fire lit with cardboard boxes and barbecue briquettes enabled us to heat up some minestrone soup and canned vegetables.

Danny had a few swigs of whisky after insistent prompting from Jack and then quickly fell asleep after our makeshift meal. Jack Davies kept on drinking.

"Sleep of the innocent that, don't you think? Can't hang much blame on that lad; working on the land. Not bright enough to be blamed for anything." He was slurring his words.

"So guilt is the preserve of the educated classes is it?" Josh probed.

"Well, you could argue that; I think so. Guilt requires conscious action, choices. Not sure Danny makes too many of those; his level of consciousness is probably just above that of an earthworm…"

"Conscious enough to save your bloody life."

"Okay, okay."

Josh looked hard at the ex 'master of the universe' then his eyes wandered to the shelves around us. 'Choices,' he thought. 'What choices had he made?'

"Plenty of choices here," Jack continued. "Admittedly less than there were a few years back. Some things missing like rice and drinks bottled overseas but the shelves are nearly full. The last bastion of Western excess consumption – the supermarket. Even to the last syllable we were still packaging stuff in plastic and throwing away a third of what we'd bought."

"We?" questioned Josh.

"You made your own choices to sit on the sidelines of society."

"I don't remember making many trips to a supermarket over the last five years." Josh was on the defensive.

"Maybe not, but I daresay you didn't live on fresh air. It's a question of degree."

"I don't think a man with a size fourteen carbon footprint has the right to criticise one who had to find shoes on a rubbish heap."

"There you go with that victim thing again."

"Fuck you!" Josh leapt to his feet and strode off down the personal healthcare aisle.

At the back of the store was a bakery section with a roof light letting in the last vestiges of the dusk. Josh sat next to one of the great ovens, cold as a corpse. 'Why did he let that guy get to him like that?' Somehow Jack Davies knew how to drive bamboo splinters up his fingernails. This is the type he had scorned when he was on the streets even though he was ready to take their 'droppings' in his collection box. The banker was hitting a nerve that Josh wasn't even aware he had. Maybe it was the inclusive 'we', attempting to mire him, Josh, in the consumer guilt, which belonged to the Jack Davies' of this world. It's one thing to spend your life on the streets but to then have your 'share' of blame dumped on your shoulders, your share of this mess, was like the priest punished for unworthy thoughts he never got to act on. Was that it? Unfairness?

His thoughts went back to his father. A successful barrister who became a High Court Judge. Josh accused him of bringing work home with him when he put the teenager in the dock over his performance at school. It seemed the grades were never good enough for his father whatever amount of studying and revision Josh did. When he got into the exam room it all seemed to go out the window. His father hadn't even bothered to call him the day the 'A' level results came out. He'd already written off a legal career for Josh.

The rows used to be fierce as his father defended the establishment view against Josh's furious and righteous teenage attacks. His mother stood on the sidelines unsure which loyalty to favour, her heart breaking as the divide widened. Then suddenly after the 'A' level exams came a summer of indifference as his father realised that his son would not be following the family way to Cambridge and the law. The rows petered out into the distance.

Things had continued going downhill at University. The student loan his mother had underwritten mostly went on booze and dope each month. One meal a day in the refectory kept body and soul together but the alarm in his mother's eyes when she visited him mid-term haunted him. He'd met a few other freshers in the first few weeks but they soon lost interest in him as he disappeared into his room in the halls. Guest appearances at tutorials gradually diminished until the day the message pushed under the door by the caretaker said, "The Warden would like to see you at

9.00 a.m. tomorrow in his study."

He still had the note and his students union pass in his otherwise barren wallet. It was getting cold. In the corner was some plastic sheeting, which had wrapped a pallet of floor sacks. He pulled it out straight, wrapped it round him and lay in the foetal position alongside the big oven. Maybe there he would find at least the memory of warmer days.

\*

Jack woke with a start. Where was he? He strained to remember; some hotel room? No, too cold. All around was blackness, a claustrophobic black tar cocoon of night. He pulled the sleeping bag up around his chin.

The supermarket. He remembered the food and whisky. What time was it? He looked at his wrist; nothing. He'd lost his watch when he fell in the floodwaters.

A sound. What was that? To his left a low growling noise. Maybe fifteen, twenty feet away. Christ, what was that?

His body stiffened.

The growl was getting louder. An animal; a dog? Just a dog, maybe. Must have followed us in looking for food too. What kind of dog makes a noise like that?

He tried to shout, but his throat was dry and unwilling. Shit! Where are the matches; light something, scare the hound off. Where had he put them. His rucksack lay under his head as a pillow. His free left arm reached round his chest and groped for the side pocket…

The growl grew louder and nearer… a box of something nearby. His hand grabbed and pulled hard launching it over his feet into the blackness in the direction of the growl. "Fuck off you bastard thing, fuck off."

"Wha'?" Danny had woken. "What's up? Why you shoutin'?"

"There's something there, over there; hear it?"

The darkness flooded around us, implacable, unyielding, nothingness. The growling had stopped.

"I heard something. I swear it. A dog, a brute of a thing, growling, over there."

"Can't hear nothin'," Danny said. "Go back to sleep, you're havin' nightmares."

"It's no bloody nightmare, I heard it, a dog but not like any dog I've heard before. If there's hounds round here they're getting pretty desperate for food by now I'll bet… Listen."

The silence was broken only by Jack's heart thumping against his chest.

\*

Dawn slowly penetrated the aisles, the low light seeping through the windows beyond the checkouts. Jack's ears had strained for sounds for what seemed hours until at last the low buzz of Danny's snoring had lullabied him back to a fitful sleep.

Two larval figures wrapped in sleeping bags slowly stirred.

Half an hour later, with cornflake packets as tinder, we had the briquettes burning again with a pan full of porridge simmering on top.

Josh appeared at the end of the aisle, rubbing his legs and buttocks to get rid of the night's numbness and aches.

"What was all the shouting last night?"

"I heard something; an animal."

"And? What kind of animal?"

"Must have been a dog; but it sounded like the fucking Hound of the Baskervilles. How come you didn't make an appearance?"

"I don't have night sights on these specs man. Anyway, I heard Danny after a few minutes, reckoned you were in good company. Then you stopped."

"I didn't hear nothing," Danny said.

"I'm tellin' you there was something there."

"Sure. I'm not sayin' there wasn't. Just didn't hear anything, that's all."

"Well, I'm not spending another night in this place. We haven't even got the light of the moon and stars to see by buried down here amongst the tinned beans. If there's dogs prowling around they're not going to be shy about taking a lump or two out of us. I don't see them loading up baskets with pet food and can openers."

"I think we'd better hit the road. Let's each fill our rucksacks with water bottles and as many tins as we can carry. We should keep heading North East out of town."

"And where are we heading for?" asked Josh.

"Anywhere but here," snapped Jack.

"Well, that gives us plenty of scope."

"I've got to try and find my mum," Danny said.

For a few minutes Josh weighed the options in the balance. At least here we had ready access to shelter, food and water. So what were we going in search of? It was clear Jack was going to leave; Danny would follow. So he'd be here alone if he stayed. But there was nothing very new in that. Or was there? Sleeping rough was no novelty but under the arches at Waterloo there were always the commuters and the other vagrants. Not that he had much to say to them but he could watch; something, however commonplace, happened; something to take your mind off things. What would he do if he stayed here in the supermarket other than go quietly mad like some latter-day Robinson Crusoe?

No, he'd go along with these two. Something might turn up.

# CHAPTER 6

## CONFLICT

We retraced our steps back towards the railway embankment, our best chance to get across the vast moat that surrounded the town.

Above us telephone wires sagged, stretched by the weight of a million conversations, now empty, silent, waiting. The streets echoed to our footfall, our isolation bouncing off the sides of the buildings.

"Show me on here where your home village is Danny," Jack said in schoolmaster tones, opening out the road map of Essex he'd rescued from the supermarket.

A few moments later Danny was pointing at the name Maldon.

"I would guess we're something like thirty, forty

miles from there," Jack said.

"You're not serious." Josh made one more attempt at resistance. "It'd take us five days or more at this pace assuming we don't have to swim most of the way. We'd be heading into worse flooding I'm betting. Essex is flat, man, and there's nothing to get in the way of the tidal surge. It doesn't make sense."

"Well that's where I'm heading. Don't care what you say. If it were your mum out there what would you do? I can't just give up on her like you're sayin' I should. What sort of bloke are you?"

"I'm just saying we are heading into deeper trouble. How do you know she's still out there anyway? People will have been evacuated early from all the low-lying areas particularly ones close to the coast or rivers; stands to reason. She could be anywhere by now," Josh responded.

"Not so long ago, accordin' to you she was dead; now she's evacuated. You don't know what you're talkin' 'bout. Anyway, I'm headin' home."

"Sounds as good a plan as any to me," Jack broke in. "It's a toss-up whether to go north, south, east or west. We don't know what we'll find. Maldon is as good a target as any as far as I'm concerned. We have to make for somewhere, I know that for sure."

We found the railway embankment again. Other than the crunch of boots on gravel, the world was silent as we retreated into a solipsist, inner space.

Danny's mum had said to him months back, "You watch Danny; the world's a changin' and changin' fast. Them rich folk who makes their livin' high on the hog from wheelin' and dealing are goin' ta join us scratchin' a livin' soon. Their games in the City are gonna come to an end. And then they are going to have to learn how to do without. At least the likes of us have had some schooling in that Danny, haven't we? We're all going to have to find ways of putting food in our mouths; working the land in some way, I'm guessin'. That's where you'll have the beatin' o' them Danny. Them big hands of yours, like shovels. You could work the earth with 'em, if you 'ad to. And you know how to grow things; you'll be the one who people is makin' up ta then Danny, oh yes. The changes might not be all bad if they give people like you a new start."

Danny looked around. To left and right the muddy brown waters. Even rivers don't survive when the world is awash like this. They lose their identity, their path, too.

He wanted to believe what 'Mum' had said; but he

couldn't work the land when it was covered with water. What would happen when what was left in the supermarkets had gone? There must be lots of other people out there like the three of us, scavenging for the leftovers from the 'old' world. The old world where the shelves never emptied; where folks around the world worked in sun and rain to grow things, so ships and lorries could carry them half way round the planet to go into some housewives shopping basket and grace the tables of swish London restaurants.

He'd always thought it strange that England couldn't grow everything it needed to eat. Miles upon miles of wheat, barley, oats. Thousands upon thousands of cows and sheep his mum said there were to be found across the English countryside, but never enough to feed the mouths of England. He wondered how come these other countries could spare their food. They grew stuff for 'export' his teachers had said in his Geography class. What did those folks eat? There were hundreds of millions, billions of them. More people than drops of rain on a spring day. Yet they worked in the fields to keep the shelves filled here in England, and in America and France and all those other places he and they had never been.

But now those folks were growing stuff to feed

their own families; and anyway, how were those trucks going to deliver to supermarkets when the roads were flooded and nothing was working any more. No electricity, no petrol, no people.

# CHAPTER 7

What if everybody had been drowned in the flooding? What if all the bridges in England had bodies stacked up against 'em? What would life be like then? He was used to being alone most of the day. Working in the gardens he'd sometimes see folks who lived there just to nod to and say 'g'day'. He'd often not see a soul for hours until he got back home to Mum in the evening. But this would be different. Nobody, 'cept these two fellas who he hardly knew. How long they would stick around he didn't know, but they weren't going to fill all this space he could feel inside him right now.

His thoughts turned again to when the floodwaters hit, hearing screams in that blackness and the lashing rain. He had lost consciousness at some point. Didn't know how he'd managed to stay afloat whilst the world turned upside down and inside out like some tumble wash.

His head was like that tumble wash now. Thoughts reeling and jigging like socks and shirtsleeves, intertwining, flailing around for something. Some anchor. Some reason to keep walking this railway line.

When you're marching towards some destination, some place you're headed to, then you can measure your progress. Whether it's a hundred miles or a thousand, each step takes you closer to the objective. The journey may be hard going but your legs know there's some reason for it and you can imagine what it will be like when you arrive.

Jack Davies was used to having goals; many of them short run, close to hand; but when reached, there was always another to take their place.

But this walk wasn't like that. Somewhere, sometime ahead we would find another settlement, a village or town. Our rucksacks were full enough to keep us going for maybe a week or more but eventually we would need to find new supplies of food and water. So wasn't that enough reason to carry on? If that was the reason we might as well have stayed in that supermarket. There was enough there to keep us going for months, a year or more. No, it couldn't just be about staying alive for now, for tomorrow. One day the shelves would have been empty, then what? Then we would have had to move, to find someplace else. And what would have happened in the intervening months? Would other survivors have appeared at last, also looking to find enough food to eke out their existence, their stay of execution? Would we have fought over the remaining contents of those shelves or shared? He was glad not to have had the answer to that question, yet.

But what would count as 'arriving', now. Finding other people? Maybe. Finding out what had happened? How far had the flooding gone? Was it just Essex and the Thames Estuary or wider? Where had everybody fled to?

The water shimmered in the mid-afternoon sun. Treetops stuck out as if struggling for air. A breeze made a washboard of the surface. This was what must have greeted Noah after the rains. Implacable, indifferent, washing away everything that had gone before.

All the things men had built to make sense of the world, to keep the chaos at bay, all would be dumb and silent now. Electricity generators, telephone exchanges, sewage treatment works, water pumping stations, roads...

Would they rebuild these things? Who were *they*?

Government? It would cost hundreds of billions even if it's only East Anglia that's been hit. And where was Government now? The House of Commons was at least waist deep in water. They had announced that essential administration services were being relocated as part of the evacuation contingency plans but he'd left town before the final announcements. New Orleans was left for a long time to try and drag itself out of the mud until pressure built up on federal government. But the circumstances were different now. There would be many New Orleans and worse, if the climatologists were to be believed. They couldn't rebuild everything. Just like the Wash and the Fens, they'd surely have to retreat, retreat to higher ground and surrender the past to the waves, the rising waters.

What then? City-states on hilltops?

Josh Stieglitz had long since given up on the job, mortgage, wife and kids solution to life's meaning and purpose. He'd spent his teenage years and early twenties scorning the establishment and everything it held dear, and he wasn't going to swap that for a comfortable life, even if he could. The longer he slept rough, the harder it was to conceive of life being otherwise. How could he turn his back on the months of deprivation? That would be to dishonour the streets and the other lost souls who made their homes there wouldn't it? Or so the pride in him still argued. When you've gone so far, it's defeat, shame, to turn back. No, he had made his choice and sticking with it was the only hope of being right; and being right still meant a lot to Josh Stieglitz.

"You suppose you have a choice?" asked a familiar voice in his head.

"What?"

"Well, you assume society would let you in if you knocked on the door. Why should it? What have you got to offer? A University dropout without any profession or trade. How exactly do you expect to get a job, to get a life?"

His father's voice again beat the bass drum of doubt.

Maybe he was right. He, Josh, had a habit of denying the things he most wanted. If you don't admit to wanting something then you can't be disappointed, can you? If you don't play the game, don't compete, you can't lose. If you don't love, you can't get hurt. If you don't trust you can't be let down.

"If we live the lives our fathers want for us, we have to be perfect," he had once said to a fellow student at Nottingham. "We can never really fill the gaps, the things left undone by the last generation. So why try?"

He felt a clutch in his throat. What was that about? It was the same feeling he'd had when telling his parents he'd been sent down from University. A mixture of anxiety, remorse and shame.

"No way back now," the words shot through his head.

Lurking in the corner of his mind he glimpsed a truth, crouching ready to ambush him; ready to turn his defences over. No way back. The things you said you didn't want are gone forever. Fate has taken you at your word. So how does that feel?

"Hum," he let out an involuntary groan, as if the thoughts now crowding his skull had to find some exit valve, a way of letting out some of the pressure.

"What's wrong?" Jack Davies five metres further down the track turned round.

"Nothing. Nothing. Keep going."

"Didn't sound much like nothing," Danny said. "You ok?"

"Yeah, sure. No worries."

It's just a motherhood that you don't know that you want something until you find you can't have it. Isn't it? Josh Stieglitz looked over the edge of his life at the sheer drop into the bottomless blackness. For a moment the emptiness took his breath away. Then the waves of shame came back; his heart pounded as those waves broke. "No way back."

Whether he wanted them or not, the things he had so long scorned may now be lost forever, washed away by man's greed. Washed away in the cause of human 'progress'. Ironic that such 'progress' had borne the seeds of its own end; some in-built obsolescence in man's DNA, like a light bulb. Now he felt the shoots of anger in his stomach. It was one thing for him to voluntarily abdicate from society, but quite another thing for others to throw it all away. For others to foul the nest so that it became uninhabitable even by a 'cuckoo' such as he.

We reached a viaduct spanning a wide valley with wooded sides. Below us a stream engorged with brown, silted water rushed urgently down. The railway track had gradually climbed to higher ground.

As the afternoon had worn on, dark clouds had formed and an easterly wind had stirred the oaks. We had a common goal, to find shelter and the warmth of a fire before the heavens opened again.

At the end of the viaduct there was a path turning left up an escarpment towards a copse. We decided to leave the railway track and make our way to the trees in search of firewood. Two hundred metres along the escarpment, Jack Davies suddenly held his arm up in a half-sign: "Look."

Above the trees, around three hundred metres ahead was a spiral of grey smoke.

"At last, some signs of life. I was beginning to think we'd never see another living soul. Much as I treasure your company gentlemen, the thought of spending the rest of my life with just you guys was starting to weigh on me a little," Josh said grinning.

We moved faster along the incline and then into the trees. Five minutes later we entered a large clearing in the copse and ahead stood an ochre walled house roofed with pan tiles. The welcoming smell of wood smoke filled our nostrils.

"Looks like our hotel for tonight," Jack said.

'Crack!'

"What…?"

'Crack!' A second shot split the air and splintered bark from a tree five paces to Danny's left.

"Get down, get down, they're shootin' at us," cried Danny.

"What the hell….?"

"Get down!"

The three fell to the ground, behind a rocky outcrop.

"Hold on. Hold on. We don't mean any harm. Quit firing. Just looking for somewhere warm for the night…"

'Zing, Crack.' Another shot powdered the edge of the rock above Josh's head.

"Christ! Who the hell…?"

"Stop firing for God's sake…!"

'Crack!'

"We've got to get out of here," screamed Jack.

"Stay on your bellies and crawl down behind those trees. Keep your heads down."

We followed Jack's lead, squirming backwards heads down, ears filled with the racing of our hearts. The ground fell away sharply behind us as we scrambled, knees and elbows scraping on the sharp flinty soil.

"Stop; wait a bit," ordered Jack.

The hillside was quiet. We couldn't see the house anymore; with our heads held low the ridge near the brow of the hill hid the building, but we could still see the chimney smoke, circling up against the glowering sky.

"We've got to get up and run for it. Shit knows

whether that mad man's going to come after us, but we're dead meat staying here."

"He's right," Danny said.

"On my count of three," Jack said.

We tumbled down the hillside back towards the railway track, every second of the fall expecting a lancing pain in our backs or limbs. But none came.

Looking back up the hillside, as we gasped for breath, all sign of the house was gone except the telltale wisps of smoke near the summit. We could see no one.

"A bit hostile!" Josh said searching for his sense of humour as comfort.

"We'd better get well away from here. Let's go round the hill and see if we can find a spot to camp a few miles on."

"My feet are blistered," moaned Josh.

"What do you prefer, blisters or a punctured backside?"

"No contest!"

We had been going just ten minutes when the growl of thunder reached us. Another ten, and the rain started to lash down. We found a small stand of oak trees on the hillside and crouched against the base of the largest of them, watching the rainfall like bullets. The landscape lost its form as the rain dissolved a lightless world and extinguished any hope of a warming fire. Lightning forked the sky, for moments illuminating the hillside and the tall oaks in a primeval scene.

Between each flash the world grew darker and colder as the rain soaked through to our skin. We huddled closer to the tree, wiping the rain away from our eyes, each utterly alone in his isolation.

A great flash lit up the scene again, and there, five metres away, a shape moved. Jack's body stiffened. Had the others seen it? Again the darkness fell. Just a trick of the light? He waited, not daring to move. He strained his eyes to see if he could make out the shape again, to detect any motion. He wanted to ask the others whether they had seen it but daren't make a sound.

The branches above swirled and groaned in the wind as the storm gathered its fury. The rain lashed down still heavier, flooding his eyes now.

Another flash. There, just a few paces away was a long figure, motionless, silhouetted by the lightning. Some sort of animal? What the hell was it?

Then suddenly the hillside lit up, as if under the

glare of searchlights, a great zig zag of lightning tearing open the sky. Closer now, he could see the creature; a tiger! For a moment his mind just would not accept the testimony of his senses. A tiger, on an English hillside.

The animal stood stock-still. In that flash Jack saw its cold, unblinking eyes fixed on him. Eyes that were alien, unfeeling. Eyes that seemed to look deep inside him. The animals coat was lank and soaked by the rain; ears flattened against the side of its head.

The lightning flash switched off and the blackness fell again.

That was it. That was the last thing he was ever going to see. He willed himself to get up and run but his legs made no response. Where was it? He braced himself against the tree and folded his arms in front of his chest, shutting his eyes. An eternity ticked slowly by.

Another crack and flash. He opened his eyes slowly. Gone. Where is it? It's moved away. Where is it now? Oh God!

He shot his eyes quickly left and right as the lightning crackled. Nothing. It's gone.

He became aware of his breathing, a fast shallow panting, as if he dare not fill his lungs for fear it would make the animal reappear.

It was a full ten minutes before Jack broke the silence.

"Where the hell did that come from?" he asked in whispered tones.

"What?" Josh responded.

"What do you mean 'what'? The tiger `of course. You can't have not seen it for God's sake. Must be a zoo or wildlife park in the area," Jack said.

"What are you going to spot next? A rhinoceros, a bull elephant?"

"I'm telling you there was tiger. Why do you think it left us alone?" asked Jack.

"When was the last time you heard of a tiger mauling someone in the English countryside? Hallucinations rarely bite," Josh quipped.

"There was something in its eyes," Jack said.

"I'm guessing *surprise*. What do you mean?"

"I don't know. It looked kind of... Well, lost."

"Like us?"

"I guess so."

\*

An hour passed before we dared to move. Danny was the first to stand and stretch his legs. The storm was dying now, but in the distance another bank of heavy cloud obscured the horizon. The world seemed to be liquefying.

"We can't stay here all night. I dunno 'bout you two but I'm soaked through. We got to find somewhere we can make a fire," Danny said.

A miserable hour of stumbling in the gloom later, we came upon an old farmhouse. We waited for a full fifteen minutes some fifty yards from the house to see if there were any signs of life. Jack shouted: "Hello, in there. Anybody there?" After a long enough silence he pushed open the door.

The downstairs was a single room with a large open fireplace bearing the cold remnants of a log fire. Danny found logs and tinder at the side of the great hearth.

"You've got the matches Josh," he said.

Josh felt in the side pocket of his rucksack; then felt the other side.

"Shit!"

"What?"

"They must have fallen out when we were round

that tree; that's the only time I put my sack down. Shit. How could they?"

"I don't believe it. You only took one packet from the supermarket. What is it with you?" Jack started to launch into him.

"I didn't know we were going to be wandering the Essex countryside for days without seeing another soul. How the hell was I supposed to know it was the end of the world?"

"C'mon, you two. This wood's dry. Look in the drawers over there, see what you can find," Danny interrupted.

Ten minutes later Danny was remembering his Boy's Brigade technique and drawing a flame from two pieces of flint and some cotton wool tinder. Another ten minutes and a fire was lit.

Jack continued to search the cupboards. Laying on its side on a shelf in the, otherwise empty, larder he found a radio.

He switched onto the FM wave band and turned the knob sliding the cursor over the stations. The radio just gave a crackle of static then fell silent as the bar moved on. Then something. Faint. What was it? French. Yes some French station; indistinct, a long way off but an unmistakeable Gallic tone. He could almost see the broadcaster's shoulders shrugging with resignation. But his 'O' level French could decipher little except 'hazard'... 'demonstration'...

He turned to where the gauge said BBC Radio 4, then 3, 2 and Radio 1; nothing but a low whine seemingly from another planet.

He was about to give up when on the last wind of the tuning knob he heard:

"This is Ed Shaw on Radio Essex. For anyone just joining us, we are taking calls from listeners around the Region updating on how things are in the county. We have been informed that senior civil servants and some members of the Cabinet have relocated to an undisclosed location in the Home Counties. A National State of Emergency has been declared. TV and the main Radio stations are not currently broadcasting but some mobile phone networks are still operating intermittently though with increased black spots.

"Some of our callers have been in touch with friends and family overseas. I'm afraid you will find much of this news distressing but if you can please bear with us; if you have information you think will add to the emerging picture of how things are across the UK and beyond then please call in if you can. Call on this number 0800 777 100 that's 0800 777 100. I'm Ed Shaw."

"We have another caller on the line. Who's calling please?"

Pause.

"Hello. This is John Thatcher… in Braintree. We're surrounded by water here. It hit us six days ago, during the night, an enormous surge, flooded halfway up the windows on the ground floor. We were upstairs in bed, thank God."

"How are things now John; is the water going down; how are you coping?"

"No, it doesn't seem to be. We managed to get some bottled water. My son David swam to the local store. But that's getting low. It's dangerous going over there now; some pretty desperate people around. We rescued some cans of fruit and beans from downstairs but that's all we have. Where the hell are the emergency services, the Army or somebody? Isn't somebody supposed to help get us out of this mess?"

"No one has tried to move you out to safer ground?"

"No. We haven't seen anybody. Some of our neighbours have shouted across the streets; we've tried calling 999 endlessly; no response. Some others are…"

Pause.

"Some others what… John?"

Pause.

The caller's voice seemed to dissolve; then a sobbing sound. "… Some of the other people round here… bodies in the water… didn't make it."

Pause.

"I'm… I'm so sorry John."

"Where the hell are the authorities; surely somebody is on the case? More folk down here are going to die without access to clean water. David's a strong swimmer. He's been out to the edge of the village, but he said there was just water as far as the eye could see; and no sign of any rescue services. Where are the boats, the helicopters, man? Can you get a message to them, to someone…?"

"We'll try John. We have an emergency number, but haven't had any success yet in getting through. The landlines seem to be down; must be flooding in the exchanges. Our backroom people keep trying through the mobile networks. I'll give you the number in case you have better luck. It's 0800 222

111. Repeat… 0800 222 111. Can I make a plea to any members of the emergency services listening to this broadcast; could you get in touch on the following number… 0800 777 100; that's 0800 777 100. We need to hear from you; to hear what's being done to help people stranded by the floods. People need to know what to do and what to expect."

The broadcaster's voice sounded ragged, husky as his own fear threatened to get the upper hand.

"Christ, this is wider spread than I thought. Braintree is, maybe forty, fifty miles from here. How much flooding can one tide create?" asked Jack Davies.

"Maybe the heavy rains, you know, run-off in the towns with nowhere to go," offered Josh.

"Maybe. Wait…"

"Hi, you're through to Ed's phone-in. What's your name please?"

"Charlotte. Thank God I got through," an elderly lady's voice tremored over the airwaves.

"Welcome Charlotte, what's your situation?"

"I'm in my car. Been here for days now on Copse Hill. Where is everybody? I thought someone was sure to arrive by now. The nights are cold and I'm running out of water. I always carry a big bottle in the boot, but it's nearly empty. Can you help me? Get someone to get me out of here. I've tried walking out but always reach floodwaters; seems like I'm surrounded, on an island. Isn't someone looking for stranded people?

"We're not sure what's happening right now, Charlotte. Try to stay tuned and as soon as we have news we'll put it out on the air.

"My house is down near the river. I don't know what's happened; it's three miles away, I can't get back; don't know what to do. And my dog, Benjy, is in there. Oh, I hope he's alright. He's all the family I've got now…"

"Charlotte. Charlotte are you there?"

The radio went quiet.

Jack took hold of the aerial and twisted it around.

"… Charlotte. Looks like we've lost Charlotte for the time being. If you are still listening, my dear, keep tuning in and we'll put out news as soon as we have anything, anything at all."

"Turn it off for God's sake," Josh said.

"It's about the only way we're going to find out what's happening," Jack retorted.

"The guy hasn't got a clue; isn't that clear enough?"

Jack leant over and turned the on/off knob, saying: "Fine, let's just stay in the dark, shall we? We need to get some idea of where to head to. We'll be out of food and water again in a few days unless we find some fresh supplies."

"You were the one who said we had to leave the last town. The supermarket seems like a good place to be right now," Josh retorted.

"If you want to back track that's fine by me."

Jack flicked the 'on' switch again between index finger and thumb. "… we've got family near Bristol; we called them on the mobile. They said a huge wave came up the Bristol Channel and Severn estuary. Houses along the estuary have been swept away. There's no electricity and no mains water. They got out ok, somewhere near Clifton now, but they say that people are looting shops to get food and water."

"Thanks, Richard. Any other callers out there?"

Pause.

"Call in on. 0800 777 100. Let us know how things are in your area."

"Anyone?"

Silence.

"We'll stay on the air as long as we can; as long as

the standby generator here has fuel."

"Where's 'here' for Christ sake; tell us where you're broadcasting from you fool," Jack was shouting at the radio now.

"I'm guessing many of you have lost your mobile phones in the flooding, or… maybe some of the networks are down. If you can get through tell us whether you have seen any evidence of the emergency services in action or have any other contact numbers people can use." There was a note of desperation in Ed Shaw's voice.

Jack turned the radio off again. "Better conserve battery power; don't know when or where we might find out any more," he mumbled a half-hearted explanation.

"Well at least we know there's some other folks alive out there," Danny said. He thought of his 'mum'.

"I'm not sure we are in the majority though," Josh said, without a trace of humour in his voice.

*

"Why is it you two don't like each other," asked Danny.

"What do you mean?" asked Jack, defensively.

"Well, you are always arguin' and the like, aren't you?"

They looked at the floor.

"Different world views, I guess," Jack mumbled.

Josh was squatting on his haunches by the fire tenderly administering to the flames, putting on twigs and bark to feed it.

"World what?" asked Danny.

"Just have a different idea about what's important, about how a man is supposed to live his life," Jack continued.

"And what's your idea?" Danny persisted.

Jack drew in a deep breath then exhaled slowly.

"Right now I'm not sure anymore. A few months ago it seemed pretty clear. Work hard and play hard. Doing the next deal was enough, enough to make me feel like I had a place in the world. It seemed like somebody had to do it and I was, am, good at it. Maybe that's all any of us can ask, to find something we're good at."

"I see," Danny said, thinking he didn't.

"Well, if you do maybe you can explain it to me," Jack continued. "I guess the money was a big part of it. While that was piling up in the bank account, I felt, well… I felt I was somebody, somebody making good in the world. Isn't that how we measure success after all?"

"I never had much money. Most of what I earned went to Mum to pay the rent and for food. I kept my van going though; needed that to get round my customers."

"So maybe you had everything you needed then," Jack said.

"Not sure about that," Danny said. "How do you know when you've got enough?"

"Our economy is based on the principle that there is never enough. If people stop wanting new things, more holidays, eating in more expensive restaurants, new houses, second cars, then the whole thing grinds to a halt."

"Why?"

"Well, that's just how economies work." Jack floundered for a few moments. Somehow the words are difficult to find when you are asked to explain the self-evident, axioms of one's life, and to do so in a way someone like Danny can understand.

"Basically, people wanting and spending more means there are more things that need to be produced, more goods and services. That, in turn, creates jobs for people, so we can earn money and we too can consume products and services. That way the economy grows, companies make profits, which they reinvest creating more jobs providing pension incomes for those too old to work. Those companies and individuals pay taxes on our incomes so that the Government can spend on things society as a whole needs but which most individuals, couldn't afford by themselves. Things like health services, police, armed forces, roads."

"What happens when you get to the point where people have got enough of all those things?"

"Well, that's not necessarily a good thing, Danny. If people stop buying things other than the basics then the economy stops growing."

"And then what?"

"That brings problems. The population keeps on growing as long as people keep living longer and we have two point two children per couple. Add immigration to that and each year there are more mouths to feed. Unless the rest of us are going to keep those extra people in food and lodgings then they too will need to get jobs, making things and providing services. We need customers for our services and if the rest of us say we'll stick as we are, we don't need any more', then the new jobs just won't be created. Unemployment grows and so on."

"And so on?"

"You ever been out of work since you left school?"

"Yeah."

"Did you get bored?"

"Yes."

"And how did that feel?"

Danny thought for a few moments.

"Like I was bad, useless."

"Exactly. You get millions of people feeling like that and you've got big social problems. The devil makes work for idle hands.

"So, as long as we've got more people in the world each year we all have to keep consuming more things otherwise we get into a bad place," summarised Danny.

"That's about it," Jack confirmed.

"So, we shouldn't ever be satisfied with what we've got or otherwise the economy stops working and we end up with lots of miserable people?"

"Hmmm," Jack said.

"We have to keep consuming more, and working harder to keep the show on the road," Josh continued.

"That's your idea of how things are supposed to be?"

"I guess that's how I see it."

"But some people get miserable when they see that other people have got more than they have. Mum is a bit like that. She used to…" Danny paused.

"She used to get angry that we had so little when there was all those folks in the City living it up."

"That's just inevitable. There's always going to be differences between people, differences in skills and the kind of jobs they can do; just plain luck sometimes. But on average we're better off as the economy grows, and the tax system and government spread the wealth around."

Josh had continued to tend the fire, listening and taking pleasure at first in hearing Jack digging himself into a hole.

"Ask him how come we're sat here having to light a fire to dry our clothes, given the marvels of our modern economy, Danny. Ask him, how come all this human progress has left us living like some Neanderthal tribe, rubbing sticks together. I'd be interested in the answers," Josh finally snapped.

The anger was never far below the surface.

Moments passed.

"I don't see how you can blame Jack for that," Danny said, at last, "It's not as if he whistled up the rain and the floodin'. He might have been a powerful bloke in the City but he's not Moses."

"C'mon Danny," Josh replied. "What started all this climate change stuff? Jack Davies' view of the world is just what has kept the US and every other developed nation spewing out $CO_2$ and using up the resources of the only planet we've got. Then along come India, China and the rest saying you've had your run now it's our turn and three more billion people join the global consumer society – all of us with chimneys on our heads."

"I knows that stuff but one man doesn't cause all that," replied Danny. "What could one man do?"

"Yeah, but a 'world view' does, a world view shared by Jack Davies' kind. A view that we can trash the planet 'cos we won't be around to take the consequences. A view that says we have to keep this merry-go-round spinning so we can make our big bonuses and then fuel the next ride...

"See Danny – Josh and me are never going to see eye to eye," Jack interrupted. "Josh has an alternative economy, one based on wandering the streets and begging for the next meal. Somebody who does that with his life is never going to understand the aspirations of the human race, is he…"

At that moment Josh leapt to his feet and flung himself headlong in Jack's direction, hitting the ex-banker in the midriff with his shoulder and tumbling over with him onto the floor.

"Shit. Get off you asshole…" screamed Jack. Josh's arms continued like an epileptic windmill until Danny's great shovel hands grabbed him under the armpits and ripped him away from the dazed banker.

Immediately Josh felt Danny's strength, his body sagged and slumped as Danny held him, hands clasped across his chest. Josh gasped for air, his chest heaving in Danny's tight embrace. Then the sobbing started. Low at first, hesitant, unsure, then growing into a keening and wailing Danny had not heard since that day his mother had said goodbye to Danny's father.

Danny held Josh's limp body as the heart and soul of the man poured out.

Jack lay still on the floor watching the scene. Unsure whether to feel anger or compassion and unable to find either.

The three hung, frozen in space and time.

Finally, Danny relaxed his grip and Josh fell gently

to the floor.

The evening passed in silence, each lost in his own thoughts, until the light faded.

Finally, Danny spoke.

"Listen, the pair of you. I don't want no part in any more of your arguments. There's been somethin' goin' on between the two of you since we met. I don't know what it's about, but it don't make any sense to me. People who should be worried about how we goin' to find enough food 'n water to keep body 'n soul together don't have fights over 'world views'. It don't make any sense. Maybe you knows what it's about but I don't, and I don't care anymore. I reckons I'd be better off on my own. For all we know we could be amongst the last handful of people left alive in all this mess. I don't know right now whether we should be thankful for that or not. But what I do know, is you two had better start showin' each other some respect or I'm going off on my own.

"Somewhere out there my mum's on her own, God bless her, and you two are fightin' like overgrown kids. If she were here, I can tell you, you would feel the flat of her hand. Whatever led us here we only have each other right now. No-one else."

The two adversaries said nothing. Danny's words

carried an uncomfortable truth. Like it or not, this was the only team around. We made a go of it together or we were on our own. All of us lay awake for an hour or more in our sleeping bags, feeling the precariousness of this new existence before sleep finally claimed us.

# CHAPTER 8

## SEA

I don't recall how we got there. No sighting from a distance or smell of ozone in the air. No scrambling down cliffs. We just sort of arrived. Arrived with our ears suddenly full of wheeling, screeching seagulls. The road sign was draped with seaweed. The streets littered with a melange of waste vomited by the big waves. Southend. Southend-on-Sea; now Southend-under-sea; a modern-day Atlantis but not one bathed by the benevolent, azure seas of the Aegean. Pools of dirty brown foam seeped, oozed, inseminated, rotted, stank in its smothering embrace this once upon a time rollercoaster, fish 'n' chips, B & B, salty aired, working class, holiday haunt.

We walked through the town in the direction of the promenade but soon found ourselves at the water's edge. Road signs stuck out of the grey-brown dishwater sea. Houses showed the high-water mark three feet higher as a dark stain along the white pebbledash. The level had fallen but still covered the promenade to a depth of four or five feet. Waves lapped at our feet as if trying to claim us, to take us to that deep place of all the lost souls caught by that first tidal surge.

To our left a boat at 45° resting on its keel thrown up by the burgeoning seas and now hundreds of yards from its native environment, helplessly stranded like a beached whale. The letters RNLI on its bow spoke of hopelessness in the face of nature's fury. A fury like that of a hornet's nest disturbed, like mother nature, as a woman scorned by man's hubris.

The fairground Ferris wheel peeped like a half moon above the dark surface, empty pods swinging on their axles. We could still hear the excited screams of children engraved on the wind. Had they been in mid-ride when the wall of sea hit? The feigned terror of the wheel replaced in an instant by lung filling saltwater. It must have been so fast that the brain had no time to adjust to the inevitability of death. I wanted to believe that. Just blackness and an end like a full stop, small, without duration in time just final like all ends marking the passing of something but without having any content of their own.

A noise came from one of the amusement arcades across the road; like metal on metal. The sound got louder and more familiar as we entered the gloom of the arcade. As my eyes adjusted I could make out a hunched figure sat on a barstool. He reached out to the arm of a one-armed bandit and 'chunk, whirr' set the barrels spinning. Clunk, clunk, clunk, they came to a stop. The figure sat motionless then reached up again to set the barrels spinning once more.

"Hi," Jack broke the silence. The figure spun round. Two piercing blue eyes stared out from under a hood.

"Hi," Jack tried again. "We don't mean you any harm. Just thought we'd look around town for food and fresh water; do you know…?"

The man turned away, through $90°$, and took up his vigil over the machine. His arm levered down and spun the barrels yet again.

"Just wondered if you knew of anywhere…"

"Two fucking bananas and an apple…"

"What?"

"Two fucking bananas and an apple. Fucking rotten fruit come up time and again. This 'ere machine is bent. At least it's workin' without me 'avin' to put in more coins. But I been at this for hours, no days, I don't know how long, and you think I had one break? Nah, not a chance, it's rigged I tell yer. No one ever got poor owning one of these places. Daylight robbery it is, should be reported to the authorities for tamperin' with the machines. No way are these things straight; some jiggery pokery."

"Let's go," Jack said, "this guy's lost it."

"Shouldn't we take him with us?" asked Danny.

"He doesn't want to go anywhere. Here playing the machine is as good as it gets for him."

We walked back slowly up the High Street, the sound of the barrels spinning gradually fading behind us. Buckets and spades, beach balls, cricket balls, a stump, kites, strewn amongst the silted sand lying across pavement and road and clogging the storm drains.

Everywhere the contents of shops and homes flushed out by the sea. I had seen this only once before in the pictures of the Asian Tsunami in 2004 on our TV set. It's like the water, a burglar looking for valuables, rushes into every crevasse with its fingers ripping out chairs, tables, chests of drawers and scattering their contents like confetti. All the personal belongings of this seaside community exposed, left beached up or floating, mingled by the sea: picture frames robbed of the family photo; clothes mangled by the waves; kitchen chairs; bedding wrapped around smashed pieces of furniture, pillows floating like the bodies we saw at the bridge. Neighbours had never been so intimate as in their absence.

But no people, not even the dead kind. The town must have been evacuated before the waves hit. Maybe it was more obvious that the coast would suffer. But they didn't imagine the surge would go up the river systems. And that failure of imagination had probably cost more lives than we dared to think.

We turned to take one last look at the town and the brooding sea from the top of a sandy cliff. The wind blew hard, frothing the sea into white horses and stinging our face. Overhead, gunmetal skies scudded relentlessly.

Danny had told us that he was twenty-six. He was a powerful figure with legs like tree trunks and forearms which seemed to be knitted from steel cables. His brown skin was seasoned by a dozen years in all weathers shaping nature in the gardens of the Suffolk well-to-do. He owed his lantern jaw to his mother and Norfolk stock. His father had left so early in his memory Danny could not, or would not lay claim to any legacy of features from that quarter. Grey-blue eyes scorched out from under black bushy eyebrows and sat above a nose misshapen by a blow from man, beast or machine in some undisclosed incident in Danny's past.

The whole added up to a manly boy with an innocent, wide-open face, a face not yet lined by the disappointments and let-downs of a fully lived adult life. Along with that innocence was an uncertainty, a hesitation that was in the habit of awaiting approval before acting. Deeper still in those eyes was a hurt, a raw unresolved, original hurt which watched protectively and was ready to walk away rather than take the risk that other people pose.

On the edge of town we saw a Victorian school and its tarmac playground.

\*

I rubbed the dust off the windows, made a circle with spit to look through. The desks and chairs were in neat rows as if the caretaker at our old junior school had been there. He liked to have us look tidy – Mums like that too. The blackboard was empty with white sweeps just showing where the board duster in Mrs Riding's windmill hands had rubbed out yesterday's lessons. I feel; what do I feel? Sad, I think. Wait, now I can hear something. Chairs moving, feet on floorboards. We're coming in; it's morning and registration. There's Richard Johnson, big head, always showing off, makes me sick. With Diana Ratcliffe. Always got his paws on her. There, at the front. Me. Why did Mrs Riding make me sit at the front? Everybody's looking at me. I'm sticking out like a sore thumb, a big lad up there. I try to keep my head down and shoulders slumped to be as small as I can but that Johnson jerk still says things and the others laugh around me; I go red, my cheeks hot, everybody can see.

Mrs Riding tells us to be quiet. She's old and we listen to her, at least most of the time we do.

"Get out your history books," she says. Desks open and everybody fishes around. I can't find mine. No, I left it at home. What'll I do? I keep the desk lid up so Miss can't see me, my hand rustling the books knowin' the one I want is on the kitchen table at home. Around me the desk lids are barking shut – I have to do something. Geography. My Geography book's the same colour; maybe she won't notice. I pull the exercise book out and close the lid quietly.

"Now go to your project on Queen Elizabeth and finish labelling up the picture of the Golden Hind."

What to do? I feel sweat on my forehead, wipe it and wipe my hands on my trousers. Get my pencil out. Miss is walking over to the window side of the room. She walks slowly up and down aisles looking at others as we start.

"Danny," she says, 'what are you…?"

Suddenly I'm back outside looking in. Back in the rotting streets. Back with the others. It's me, big Danny, the grown-up Danny. It happens sometimes. Like I slip through time to before; to before I left school; to when I was a little 'un. Don't know why or what makes it happen but it's not nice – always seems like I end up someplace where little Danny is unhappy.

\*

We were about two hours outside of Southend. I'd strayed off the path a bit when it happened. The grass was long and wet. I enjoyed the refreshing feel against my legs and the smell; the smell is well… alive, unlike anything else I'd come across in the last weeks and months. I think the others were walking ahead, feet crunching on the path. I've started to speed up when my leading leg fishes for the ground in front but finds only air. It seems to drag me over in a clumsy cartwheel; my arms start to flail in the hope of catching some anchor but I am falling, falling through the earth; now my head and shoulders are leading the way and darkness falls. I'm falling, faster. Then I bounce against something. My hands grab, claw. My fingernails fill like spades and still I fall until suddenly I hit solid earth and the wind is squeezed out of my chest. I feel a dull smack on the back of my head and a warm sticky something running down my neck. Then… just silence.

It must be only a few seconds, or minutes, but there's no telling. Looking up I see a white space above my head. Maybe fifteen feet away. Gradually a blue sky patched with white clouds resolves in the space. Then one, two dark round shapes eat into the sky disk. Two heads, shouting; shouting: "Josh…" It takes a while to remember who and where I am, and as each fragment fits back together I hope for some other reality, some other time. But this is the only one available and it was too persistent to be switched off by a simple fall and knock on the head.

"You alright Josh?" It was Jack's voice. There seemed to be a note of concern.

"Yeah," I reply, "no bones broken." I try standing and slip back against a wall of earth. My eyes are coming to terms with the gloom. I am leant against a bank of earth. Under my feet is a wet stone, limestone. I look up as if to refuel my eyes with light, then look back down around me. The darkness is only interrupted by the strange amoeboid dust motes on the surface of my cornea.

Gradually a high cavern takes shape with organic, flowing rock formations occasionally glistening as a shaft of light from above finds its way down into this nether region. I am lying on a ledge below which seems to be endless darkness.

I try to stand again but my leg gives way at the knee joint and I feel a throbbing pain.

"Shit."

"What's wrong?" asks Danny.

I take a few seconds. Somehow there's nothing more irritating than when someone asks 'what's wrong' as if you're supposed to know the answer and you don't. I need all my focus, all my attention on me and trying not to give in to whatever's wrong with my leg rather than being diverted to calming someone else's worries. When people ask, 'are you alright?' they are thinking of their own selfish skins and what are they going to do if things aren't 'alright'.

"Hurt my knee."

A few seconds pass. I hear Danny say something

to Jack but can't make out the words.

"Can you stand up?"

"Not sure; my leg gave way just now."

"Do you think you could climb out; there are some hand holds just above your head," asked Danny.

"I think standing comes before climbing don't you, least it was when I was a nipper," I answer, irritation now gushing out.

"Just take your time."

My head is beginning to hurt now. I trace the blood up to a matted section of hair and wince as I touch the wound.

The day outside had cleared to a blue sky and warm sun as we were walking. Now the sun is shining through the hole, like a stage spotlight, bathing me in light. The ledge is wide, around 20ft by 10ft made of limestone covered with dark brown soil, moss and lichen. My watch says 2 p.m. Darkness falls at 4.30 this time of year. I don't fancy a night down here. What if I rolled off the ledge into the bottomless pitch black? No thanks.

"You gotta get me out of here," I shout up at the two heads peering down.

One of them mumbled again.

"Speak up, I can't hear you."

"We need to get a rope that'll reach you. We have to go back to that shopping area, find a washing rope or something like that to tie round you."

"What's this 'we' business? It doesn't take two of you. You're not both going to go leaving me here!"

As soon as the words are out I'm conscious that I don't have a great bargaining position from which to start laying down the law.

More mumblings above.

"Jack will stay here; I'll go back. I'm faster than him and we want to get you out before nightfall. We've got to find a place to shelter for the night, it's going to be a cold one," Danny said.

Seconds later, I hear the gravel path scrunching with heavy boots.

Then quietness; just the sound of my breathing, irregular, first shallow then sucking in air, then shallow again. The more I focus on my breathing the more irregular it is. Like something watched becoming self-conscious, unable to find the automatic rhythm we rely on second to second, minute to minute; the rhythm that beats out life in the background whilst the foreground of our minds is filled with all the clutter of consciousness.

It's like trying to tame an excitable dog; I control my exhalation and then my inhalation, timing each rise and fall of my chest, seeking that habitual automatic gear. Panic is just a wafer-thin layer of habit away.

I look up for some reassurance that the hole in the sky is still there; that Jack is still there. The blue seems darker now and the spotlight has moved a few inches to my left, leaving me cut off at the knees. I am the centre of a sundial.

I feel the clutch in my throat when I see there is no head peering over the side. "Jack, Jack, you there?" My voice croaks. I curse under my breath. If he is there I don't want him getting the upper hand, sensing my panic.

"Jack!"

A ragged ball of hair surrounding an oval face pushes into the sky disc.

"What's up?"

"Nothing. Thought you'd gone." I hated myself as soon as those words were out.

"Gone where? Where am I going to go?"

"No need to be a smart ass about it," I say.

"Smart ass, huh. Only one 'ass' around here; the

ass who manages to find a fifteen-foot deep hole and now we have to haul that ass's ass out of the hole. Good job it's not Sunday or the God-fearing types up here would be leaving you where you lie and going off to do what God-fearin' men do on a Sabbath. Come to think of it who says it isn't Sunday; we've no idea what day of the week it is now have we?"

"Okay, okay."

How did I end up here, my life hanging on the goodwill of a city suit and an imbecile gardener? What if Danny can't find any rope? They're not going to hang about or risk their necks to get me out of here. What do they need me for? If Tesco's doesn't stock a strong line able to take my weight then I'm sunk. I have a choice I guess: I can starve on this ledge or I try to climb out, climb a sheer twenty-five feet wall of crumbling chalk and mud with a busted knee.

Quiet again. Just a stabbing pain.

Maybe this is how it ends. It's as good an ending as any other I'm likely to happen on in this new world we've made. Suppose I get out of here; then what? Starvation or getting shot by one of the 'haves' trying to defend their rations from us 'have-nots'. Not much has changed really; just that now we're allowed to kill to get our way. Allowed to kill because there's nobody left to disallow it.

The sky is getting darker. I can see the evening star glimmering. The floodlight is weaker; a mixture of falling sun and rising moon. Where's Danny? He's been gone ages. It's only an hour back to that shopping mall. What's taking him so long?

"Jack," I cry.

Quiet.

"Jack!"

A scuffling sound. Then the ragamuffin's head pokes out again beyond the edge of the hole.

"What?"

I don't know what. I've got nothing to say to him. What I wanted was just to know that he was there. I'm feeling so utterly alone now.

"Why are you shouting? I was getting a few zzz's, that's all. Don't worry, he'll be back soon."

He'll be back soon. How the hell does Jack know when 'he'll be back'. But wait, there's something different here now. What is it? Just these few words are enough to make a rope for me to hang on to. Jack didn't sound like someone who had decided there was no point hanging around. Why does he need to wait for Danny and a rope He doesn't need either, but he's still there?

I move my leg to try and ease the throbbing in my knee joint. How am I going to walk if I get out of here? There I go again; I need to worry about something, anything. Strangely it seems to take my mind off the one thing I really cannot stand – the brutal, rawness and uncertainty of existence looked straight in the face.

The floodlights' disc has moved further away overlapping the edge of the ledge now; only my legs are in half-light; the rest of me has disappeared into the pitch of the abyss. I fell out of a tree once when I was a nipper. David. Yes, David Johnson, that was his name. He shot off pretty quickly. I don't know to this day how long I'd been lying there unconscious but it was getting cool and dark... like now. When I finally got home Mum gave me a backhander and screamed at me for being late home. Some kind of friend David Johnson turned out to me. He hadn't told anyone what had happened, where I was.

*

I headed back in the direction of the shopping mall. It was maybe ten miles away. Looking at the sun it was past noon but the shadows hadn't started up yet. It was going to take a couple of hours each way, even stridin' out, so dark would be fallin' by the time we get back to the others. Darkness is goin' to make things more difficult. Maybe find another torch and batteries in the supermarket. Best we can hope for is some strong washing line. Doubled up, it'd take Josh's weight. Must be twenty feet down. Amazed he hasn't broken anything, ankle or leg. We'd have had a real problem then. Jack ain't going to hang around and I can't carry somebody of Josh's weight for long. Wonder how long it'd be before Jack will give up on him and move on if we can't get him out? He talks big, but how would he be out there on his own? Funny thing, when people argue a lot, seems like they can't do without each other.

I took the sun for direction and crossed ploughed fields as the crow flies. The furrows felt like iron under the frost but my workin' boots were strong and braced my ankles. I reckoned we was going a mile every half hour over the rough ground, faster when we could use the road.

About an hour in, something white ahead at the side of the road, It was movin'; sort of flapping. As I got nearer I saw a full-grown swan lying on its side, its breast red with blood and one wing broken, the lower half bent back against the joint. The bird's head was bouncing up and down off the side of the road as it tried to pull itself up and ward me off. I have never seen such silent pain before. Standing over its flailing body I saw my reflection in the bird's eye. I reached down to grab its neck between both hands and twisted hard and fast. The bird fell motionless, its neck and head swinging like a pendulum.

It would have been a fox. I'd often seen cygnets taken by a fox but not usually a full-grown bird. Perhaps even the wildlife were feeling the panic and drive to stay alive in these strange days after the flooding. Nature doesn't take time out to protect its own very often. And yet here I was on a mission to find rescue rope for a middle class, university drop out.

I got to the shopping mall mid-afternoon. I squeezed through the automatic doors and saw the rows of foodstuffs. I remembered that the kitchenware and other hardware were over to the right and within a few minutes had found what was needed. Twenty-five metres of washing line, and a large searchlight with batteries to fit.

Reaching the exit doors to the store I heard a strange whooping and wailing. At the far end of the parking area, maybe a hundred metres away, was a group of fifteen, twenty, people running in the direction of the store, jostling with each other to get in front. I don't know what it was about them but I pulled back and decided to hide near the tills, in the well, which once seated the checkout girls. Seconds passed and the whooping and shouting grew louder until I heard hands banging on the glass doors to the store and the familiar squeal of the doors as they were prised apart. The voices were jumbled, out of breath shouts to "try that aisle," "fill the baskets," "pick only cans and water," "find something we can carry stuff in," "look for barbecue coal and firelighters."

There were three or four different men's voices and at least one woman. Some of the accents were strange, ones I'd never heard before. For a moment I thought about showing myself but something stopped me.

The scuffling sounds of people running up and down the aisles and sound of plastic bottles hitting the steel mesh of the supermarket trolleys continued for what seemed an age. Suddenly I heard a different tone – "What do you mean it's yours; we agreed we'd be sharing whatever we found – what's up with you?"

"Fuck off – get your hands off."

"Ah!! You asshole. What's your problem?"

A loud smashing of glass, followed by the sound of tins hitting the floor. I could hear the grunts of at least two of them struggling with each other, their boots scuffling on the floor: then more crashes as they fell against the shelves and scattered the contents. The noise gave me a chance to crawl to the exit door. Once through I sat on my haunches listening to the fight for a few moments until a scream split the air; and then… the words: "he's stabbed me… help someone… help he's, arrgggghhh…" A sound like soft fruit being trod under foot "Oh God, stop… for pities sake – a woman's shrill voice started and then a high-pitched screaming. I crawled a little further dragging the rope over the ground into the parking area then stood and ran as fast as I could.

I felt dirty. Don't know why. I ran down towards the water's edge at the end of town, fell to my knees and splashed the cold water over my face as I gasped for breath. Part of me felt I should have stayed and helped – how could I run away – it was like Johnston letting me fend for myself all those years ago; another part of me said no, what did I owe those people; never met them and for all I know I'd have ended up feeling the sharp stab of a kitchen knife in my back. They were all travelling together. Was this how it was: dog eat dog? At least Josh and Jack hadn't taken knives to each other. But who was to know what would happen if and when the food ran out?

But those people in the supermarket weren't people any more. They had lost the something that made them people. Crossed over a dividing line.

I don't remember anything much about the journey back to Jack and Josh, except I was thinking a fair bit. Night was falling as I saw Jack's shape leaning against a rock. He seemed surprised when he heard my footsteps crushing the heather.

"You came back?"

"Of course I came back, why wouldn't I?"

"No reason I suppose," Jack said. I tied the rope double thickness around a tree and then threw the loose ends into the hole. There was some muttering from the hole, which I couldn't quite hear. I told Josh to tie the rope firmly round his waist and then lean back with two hands across the rope to try to walk up the sides of the hole pulling his body weight up by pulling on the rope.

I was thinking: 'what price Josh would put on this washin' line?' I doubt his mother ever had any need of hanging out their washin'. A fella like him would have been brought up in a house where they paid others to do the washin' and ironin' and to do plenty of other things they 'ad no time for. Anyway his middle-class roots and education 'adn't been much use to him lately. The world's changed and a strong arm and heart is what you needs most to get through this. Josh makes me laugh and, at the same time, he makes me think. I don't rightly know if he believes any of that stuff he calls philosophy and cosmology or whether he's just 'avin' a bit of fun at our expense. But how can you take a man seriously when he's questioning everything including whether he himself exists. Seems to me there's more than enough questions and work to do in this world without inventing ones we don't need. Maybe it's a comfort to him to think about this stuff, takes his mind off other things. I could understand that.

I hears a grunting sound and earth fallin' as Josh's head appears out of the hole and he heaves himself out with a helping hand from Jack.

Josh was panting hard with the effort of it all and lay out flat on his back sucking in air as Jack lay aside him. For a moment they seemed to be one with each other. Josh's breathing stopped. I waited, expecting something. I don't know what. It lasted just a few seconds then Josh rolled over onto his side coughing and asking for a drink of water.

Soon we were back on our way following a footpath skirting the edge of woodlands.

# CHAPTER 9

## MEETING

As we entered the edge of a clearing in some woods we saw two hooded figures sat cross-legged, close to a fire. We stood still watching for a few minutes.

"Hello," Jack shouted. His voice seemed small, lost amongst the trees. The two figures spun round and scrambled to their feet, one of them clutching a walking stick.

"It's ok, we don't want any trouble. We just spotted the smoke from your campfire. Be happy to share it with you if that's ok? We need to dry off."

One of the figures reached up and pulled down the hood of his jacket, a shock of white hair tumbling out, revealing a man in his sixties.

"Who are you?" the man asked.

"I'm Jack; this here is Josh and here, this is Danny. We're travelling, I guess like you. The three of us are evacuees from London; we got caught up in the flooding."

The other figure also dropped its hood. A woman, of similar age to the man, hair gathered in a bun and an ashen complexion, looked us up and down.

The couple stood, motionless, the man still holding onto the walking stick. You could see the tension in their wiry frames. The man was dressed in a denim shirt and grey corduroy trousers fastened around the waist with a rope belt. The trousers were muddy, the bottoms turned up and tucked into thick woollen socks anchored in brown, leather hiking boots. He continued to look at us with blue piercing eyes trying to weigh us up, to decide what to do.

The woman at his side was frail, looking as if she might fall over at any moment. She wore trousers too, black and muddied with a pair of beaten-up trainers. Her top was covered by a navy-blue donkey jacket, several sizes too big for her.

"Look, we don't mean you any harm. If we had wanted to hurt you we wouldn't all be standing here like this now would we? We just want to get warm and dry off. We lost our matches in the last downpour. If we can just dry off our stuff we'll get on our way. What do you say?" Jack tried to inject a reassuring tone into his voice, watching the faces of the couple for a glimmer of trust.

"I'm David and this is my wife Jenny. We don't have anything worth stealing and anyway… what's the point. Just park yourself near the fire. I'm sorry we don't have any food to share with you; neither of us has eaten properly for days now."

Jack noted the rucksacks leant up against each other, bulging, a few yards from the fire. We sat down as near to the warmth of the fire as we could.

"Have you been travelling long?" asked Josh.

"We live in a small village about seventeen miles south of Chelmsford," David replied.

"You're a long way from home."

"It seems further, seems like a different planet."

"What are you doing here then?" Jack asked.

"We walked here from Chelmsford. We didn't have much choice. Been walking for best part of two days now. Jenny's feet are blistered so we decided to rest up here for what's left of the day and tonight."

"Where are you heading?"

"I don't know that I have much of an answer to

that question. First we need to find some food and shelter; we've been soaked to the skin much of the last few days and we've both caught a chill. When the troubles started we tried to get into Chelmsford but they wouldn't let us in."

"Who wouldn't?"

"The police and soldiers. They've got all the main entry routes cordoned off and guarded and are patrolling most of the periphery of the town."

"I don't understand. Why?" asked Jack.

"Where have you been?"

"When we left London, we got as far as Stratford and then it's a bit of a blank after that until we met walking the mainline track out of Liverpool Street…"

The woman seemed to catch her breath, then took her husband's arm fixing us with a worried stare.

"What I meant was, do you know what's been going on?" asked the man.

"Not much. I lost my mobile somewhere along the way and we haven't had any contact with anybody else in the last two weeks: We've got a radio; we found it a few miles back, but it's only got a local station on it. Sounds like most places round here got hit by the floodwaters but it's difficult to get much of a picture from what we've heard so far on the radio."

"What are these 'troubles' you mentioned?" Jack probed.

"The looting and ransacking of the villages. Nobody seemed to be in control. When several million people are on the march and fearful of how they're going to... to stay alive then you're going to have big problems aren't you?"

"You mean the people evacuated from London?"

"Not just them. There were masses of people displaced in Essex and all along the Thames Estuary. Nobody was sure what we were supposed to do. Told to leave our homes less than twelve hours before the water hit. Those who had some fuel left tried to drive but there were hundreds of thousands on foot in the storm trying to find shelter on higher ground. The emergency services couldn't cope; eventually they gave up. Some said they were told to."

"What do you mean?"

"Well, they just disappeared or so we heard. Just melted away. Now that doesn't happen unless somebody is giving orders, does it for God's sake?"

"I don't know. What else? How do you know all this anyway?"

"The BBC kept broadcasting for a few hours after the water hit. they must have had some other facilities outside the flood area that they could broadcast from. So we saw pictures, terrible pictures."

At that moment the man's wife broke down, fell to her knees and started sobbing. The man sat down beside her wrapping his arm around her shoulder.

Minutes passed as he tried to console his wife.

Eventually, as she calmed and her chest rose and fell more slowly, he continued:

"Anyway, our village and home were trashed as droves of people came through looking for food. We decided the only thing we could do was to walk into Chelmsford in the hope that the emergency services had established some refuges there, in the churches or public buildings maybe. But when we got to the outskirts we were met by police carrying guns. We were told we couldn't go into the town and when I pressed them I got the butt of a gun in my chest.

"There were some other folk around the edges of town who'd been refused entry. They were selecting who was allowed in and who wasn't, according to some criteria laid down by I don't know who."

"What kind of criteria?"

"Well, they were only letting in the able-bodied and younger people; young women were ok but if you were above, say, forty you were refused. One of the groups we met had been told by a policeman that food and water supplies in the town were limited and that only able-bodied people were being let in because…"

The man swallowed and then put his hand to his mouth as if to stifle a cry.

"… because they were most likely to survive the hardships to come and supplies had to be directed to those best equipped to help re-building."

"Re-building?"

"I don't know exactly, but I guess re-building society, communities. It's a mess out there, there are so many dead. They also told us that there had been a lot of shootings. The army had been shooting refugees; anybody trying to cross the line was just shot."

Jack thought back to the bodies log-jammed against the bridge.

"There were lots of stories going around. I don't know which ones to believe. But for sure the police and army were not letting us into that town. We met people with mobile phones who'd been in touch with family and friends further afield. It's not just along the

Thames that this has been happening. There was a massive tidal surge up the Severn. Towns right up to Gloucester have been hit. Lincolnshire, Peterborough, Cambridge, Norfolk, the Broads, the coast of Essex and the Thames Estuary all seem to be under several metres of water and as far north as East Yorkshire.

"Christ," Josh gasped.

"People were saying that there is an emergency government in place in Birmingham and that they were directing the armed forces to 'secure' cities and what remains of food supplies. I guess those police and soldiers around Chelmsford must have been acting under somebody's orders."

"What gives them the right to decide who gets food and who doesn't; who lives and who dies?" seethed Josh between clenched teeth.

"Guess the alternative is just to let people fight it out; survival of the fittest," Jack said.

"One of the people we met gave us this," said the woman. "We think one of the police must have lost it maybe in one of the skirmishes." She handed Josh a carefully folded piece of paper taken from her breast pocket.

Josh read aloud: –

*ADMIT*

1. *Healthy females below forty years of age on showing of id with confirmation of birth date.*

2. *Able-bodied males from mid-teens to forty years, confirmed by id.*

3. *All medically qualified persons on showing relevant proof of identity.*

4. *Any member of emergency or armed forces – police, fire brigade, on production of id.*

*NO ADMITTANCE*

5. *Males and females outside the above age limits irrespective of physical condition unless in categories 3 and 4.*

6. *Any persons with any form of disability or signs of illness whether temporary or chronic.*

"Bastards," Josh growled.

"We didn't make the age qualification, as you can see," David said as if in admission of failure.

"Look. Look at the bottom left-hand corner; it's dated," Josh said, waving the paper and pointing. "19 August, three months ago; well before the last storms and tidal surge. Some bloody bureaucrat drew this up months ago. They knew. The bastards knew this was going to happen. Why else would they be issuing notes like this to the security forces?"

"Maybe part of some contingency plans," Jack said.

"Contingency plans? What contingency do you imagine that makes you segregate people like this? This piece of paper would have been dynamite if it had been found just a few weeks ago. No, they must have known the flooding was a high risk and imminent. They knew that they would soon be facing real decisions about who gets in the lifeboat and who doesn't." Josh was shaking.

"Then why did they leave it so late to evacuate London?" asked Jack.

"I used to be a civil servant," David said. "In the end that's a decision that has to be taken by the government of the day, before something happens. But the machinery of government is not well suited to acting before disasters; not when the disaster would be of this scale. Government is not good at acting on inconvenient truths or hypotheses. There would be a sort of mass delusion taking hold in Whitehall when the action needed is so enormous, such an upheaval as the evacuation of London.

"Nobody is readily going to stick their neck out

and order a mass migration of people out of the capital with all that means in terms of the risk of panic, dealing with displaced millions and, for sure, lawlessness. Let's face it, they wouldn't even have acted when they did if it hadn't been for the first surge in September and the havoc along the Essex coast and Thames estuary. They must have known the flood defences wouldn't hold this time given the size of tidal surge predicted."

"So they left it to the last minute. How many people do you think got out?" asked Jack. He remembered the platform at Stratford and those accusing faces.

"We lost our electricity supply a few hours after the surge was expected to hit. The BBC was reporting there were lots of people still trying to get out of the city when we lost signal," David said.

We fell silent as the fire crackled and spat splinters like fireflies in the gathering gloom.

It was Jack who broke the silence. "I guess you two could get into town, based on those criteria," he said, addressing Josh and Danny. "I'm firmly in the 'old folks' category I'm afraid," he continued, tossing a stick onto the fire.

"Wait till they see my CV," Josh responded,

finding refuge in irony. The group fell silent again. The woman still seemed uncomfortable whilst her husband just wore a beaten look of resignation.

We joined the circle of light thrown by the fire, each of us lost in our own thoughts.

*

Josh looked like a small boy as he gazed, eyes fixed, on the fire with his head a thousand miles away. Jack felt waves of sadness lap over him, remembering his own early twenties. A time of hope, of expectation when life was full of opportunity. He had moved to London, taken a flat and found work in the back office of an investment bank. Long hours were in the DNA there, but no one complained. That's just the way it was. There was no sense of sacrifice; what else would you rather do when there were deals to be done and the senior bankers were the men whose shoes you wanted to fill? You wanted their bonuses, their cars, their country estates and even their hourglass wives. They were really holding all these things in trust for you, until you were ready, until you had paid your dues. But, most of all, you wanted not what they owned but who they were: kings, people whose word was law for the subjects around them. Kings who decided the future of markets, who bought and sold household names, who made fools of politicians.

Yet he feared nothing. Though he wanted the future so badly, and someone powerful could take it away, that was only one future, one inheritance. There were many others. With markets booming he was becoming more valuable with each month that passed. Hostage to no one, he could move to another bank with one phone call. And we knew it; just the slightest hint and the next promotion loomed into sight; the next job to be flattered by.

It went on through his twenties and thirties. This wasn't a job, it was a life; it was the fabric, the warp and weft, of his self.

He couldn't pinpoint the time when the fearlessness drained away, when he felt he was closer to the end than the beginning. The young guns came and went as he rose to the highest levels in the bank. But somehow the oxygen got thinner up there. The guys he'd joined with had left, replaced by new generations. The average age fell as he moved into his forties and the drinking buddies disappeared one by one. It was as if all the atoms in the body corporate got changed over time till one day, though the same shape, no part of the business he had joined was left.

He could still have moved, he had the reputation, but move to what? By now he was paid more money than a man like him had interests to spend it on. Move for a bigger job? He had one of the biggest in the industry; two steps back for two steps forward didn't seem a rational deal.

He looked again at Josh, trying to see his own twenty-something, lost in the blur of all those years and deals. Then suddenly he felt the horror, the emptiness. Was that what it was like? Was that how it felt inside Josh Stieglitz, or were these demons his own? How would it have been to live on the streets? To wake and realise there were eighteen hours ahead of nothingness, of uselessness. Eighteen hours when nobody wanted anything from you; when all you had to do was to find enough food to keep you going until you could curl up in cardboard again and blot out the world of pain, until it all started over again. Eighteen hours when you could slip off the edge of this world and none of its other inhabitants would note your absence. Eighteen hours when you had to look in the face of an indifferent universe and find no answer to the question 'why are you?'

Josh looked childlike, his knees pulled up under his chin, arms clasped around his legs, rocking slightly.

Jack Davies had never had to look into that void. Not until now.

The wind had dropped to just a lick of breeze fanning the leaves above our heads. The thick dark cumulus clouds of the last few days had now given way to altostratus: purple and gunmetal grey silhouettes against the deepening gold of a sunset stratosphere. The fire cracked and threw its red tongues against our faces as we sat silent, cross-legged, soaking up the warmth. A hundred metres away an owl announced the falling of night.

Later, as Josh pulled his sleeping bag up to his chin, he wondered if he should head for the city. Our rations were getting low and there was no guarantee we would find more in the next place we came to.

But why the city? What would it be like in there? He imagined the streets filled with displaced people, sleeping in public buildings or others' houses. The security forces must be rationing things. He imagined the queues to get food and essential supplies, soup lines, maybe. Not so unfamiliar all of this. The 'flood's a great leveller', his joker quipped. When it comes down to it we all have one mouth, two hands; the basics we were issued at birth are non-negotiable.

No problem being accepted in this new order.

Everybody was down and out.

He thought of his father. Where was he now? Was he on the streets too, or worse, had he been refused entry? How do you tell a High Court Judge he has no special position in society, he has no special God-given right to food and water? How do you tell him that teenage layabouts and prostitutes have as much, even more, right to be the building blocks of a new society? Why would the new society need judges; the man with the gun is in charge and the rest follows?

He came back to the question, "why would he, Josh, go to the city?" Of course he knew how things worked in cities; he knew how to feed off the crumbs from the rich man's table, but there were no rich men, now. There were no jobs, no money system. But living as a down and out needs borrowed light, like the moon needs the sun. You can't live off the giveaways of others unless they have something to give. The poor need the rich as much as being rich needs some people to be poor.

A new start? He had dropped out, failed, when the world was still spinning happily on its axis. Why would he succeed this time when things had been turned upside down? At some level, he knew he'd opted out because that was 'safer' than to try and fail.

And once you'd placed yourself at the margins it was an inevitable next step to scorn the communities from which you had excluded yourself.

Somewhere along the line, he surely would engineer another failure, another exclusion, this time from the new order. That was his script and by God he was going to play it out, wherever his father was.

Anyway, the cities would self-digest; they would run out of supplies. Then what? The ports were flooded, infrastructure down; the rest of the world was bound to be attending to its own. Ironic, all that aid funding to lesser developed nations and, now, now the shoe was on the other foot, he didn't imagine food parcels dropping from the skies out of planes marked with the national flags of Africa and the Far East.

Danny was feeling anxious. He turned over in his sleeping bag and watched the dying embers of the fire, feeling its last glow on his cheek. He wondered how come two brainy people like Jack and Josh had ended up with such different lives. It seemed like neither of them was happy; one had too much and the other too little and neither of them could forgive the other for what we had become.

He missed his mum. She was still his best friend. He'd had a mate at school. Jimmy Roberts; he was disabled. They spent all the break times together but then Jimmy moved away. After Jimmy left, he had felt like he stuck out like a sore thumb at break times. You're different when you're on your own.

He pictured the weather vane on top of the barn at old man Johnston's farm. Life was like that. The smallest breeze could blow the direction of your life round from east to west.

After 'Dad' left the world seemed both safer and more dangerous. His mum would often cry for no reason. She worried so much about the bills; sometimes she said she dreaded the sound of the letterbox. He knew he had to be strong when he left school. The neighbours said "you look after your mum, Danny; you're a big lad; you can shift some work with those big hands and strong arms of yours. She'll be relying on you a lot now." He knew they were right but it didn't stop him feeling small inside. All those smart people hadn't made the world a safer place; how was he supposed to?

He felt himself slipping again.

*

He's been out drinking again. I can smell it, a sort of sour smell... like you gets from babies sometimes; and he's rollin' from side to side as he goes towards the TV, picks up the remote and switches channels. He collapses in 'his' armchair.

Mum says nothing. I do the same; hoping he'll fall asleep.

The man on the news says, "… inflation running at 6.3% last month."

"You needn't think I'll be givin' ya more, woman. Ya must do with what ye get. A farm labourer's wages ain't goin' up any time soon. Weather's shit. Harvest worst in five years.

"We'll manage." Mum always said that.

"Manage? Manage, eh? Well, see you do. Just mek sure ma dinner's on the table woman and that lad can wear 'is school shoes till there's no soles left. Costs a bloodie fortune ta keep 'im at school. Leavin' at fourteen was good enough for me; can't see why he should be different. They fills their heads full o' stuff there and none of it's any use to man nor beast. What's he going to do? Eh? Work on the land, I'm bound. Can't see he's going to need Shakespeare for that. He just needs strong arms and a weak 'ead. He needs that alright. If he gets too clever it'll only bring 'im misery. Well, what you looking at… looking at me as if I just crawled out from under a stone. A bit more respect woman. I've a right to a bit more respect!

He'd work 'imself into a right lather then take it out on us."

I get up and mumble, "Goin' to bed."

"Aye, quite right. Get yourself off. Got to be up at seven tomorrow to get to that school of yours. I'll have been up two hours already by that time lad; just note that. Your days lyin' abed are runnin' out fast, just you mark my word."

"Leave the lad alone, please," I hear Mum say as I bolt for the stairs. It's startin' again and it won't finish till he's too tired to lift his arm and he falls asleep on the couch.

I shut the bedroom door but I know it won't keep the noises out. A wall ten foot thick wouldn't keep their noises out. It's not so much Mum's screaming; it's like she swallows the pain as much as she can, but it's 'im, 'is ragin' and shoutin' like all the days in the fields, quiet like he had built up a storm inside 'im, a storm that broke over our 'eads when he got 'ome. A storm there was no escapin' from till it blew itself out with its lashings of his belt and the thunder in his voice: "Don't ye give me cheek woman; I'll learn thee."

It goes on for what seems like hours until finally the noise stops. It's when the noise stops and it seems like the storm's over that I fear the most. The clock on my bedroom table ticks... Huh! No! I've heard that sound more times than I can remember. The third stair creaks. Then things go black and empty. All I remember is waking up in the half-light, Mum sat on my bed, tears rolling down her blackened cheeks and dabbing the pain on my bottom lip.

*

Jack lay awake most of the night trying to decide. He could stay with the others and move at our pace, whilst the rations gave out; or he could strike out on his own. He didn't belong with the others did he? We were not his responsibility. Times like this you have to look after number one. It's like emergency oxygen masks on an airplane, isn't it – you have to put yours on first if you are going to be any use to anyone else. Part of him knew he was conning himself – if he left he wasn't intending to come back.

He quietly unzipped his sleeping bag and rose to his feet. The last embers of the fire threw a bubble of half-light, enough to see the rucksacks piled together.

The world seemed to hold its breath, other than the low buzz of snoring.

After ten minutes of silent groping in the pockets of the rucksacks Jack had transferred all the food rations and water he could fit into his own sack. He slowly pulled on his waterproof and boots then, rucksack hanging from one shoulder, he started down the hill.

As he gradually got out of range of the others he lengthened his stride, cracking twigs and leaf fall underfoot. A sense of release seeped through him melting the tension in his limbs.

He didn't need the others. We just confused things. He was always better when he was clear, decisive, just got on with things, not needing to deal with the needs of others.

After two hours of walking, the sun was sending its first limpid rays above the horizon. A world of solid things gradually precipitated out of the black, liquid night.

He sat on a fallen tree trunk overlooking the estuary, still a scene of devastation. The waters a swollen brown soup carrying tree branches, roof timbers, sticks of furniture and other remains of people's lives.

The sun rose without birdsong. Surely all the birds in the world could not be dead; yet they had lost their tongues that morning.

As the minutes passed the desolation before him seemed to seep through his skin as if by osmosis, filling him with an unbearable emptiness. This was it. This was all that was left – an implacable world of grey and brown all colour shot and devoid of any purpose other than to run down the hands of the clock.

The others would be rising; finding him gone with most of the rations and cursing him.

Why should he care? There were no rules now.

Would this be his last act with other people? The last exchange with his fellow man? A selfish one? So what? There was no one to hold him to account; no one to shame him. If there was to be shame he would have to find it inside; no one else was going to catch him, denounce him. Why should he care?

But somehow it did matter. Josh would be saying, "I told you so" to Danny. Jenny and David would only ever know him as the guy who took the rations. They would hold a picture of him as a low-grade thief. A picture held so strongly in bitter minds that it would become the only reality; it would cancel any good he may have done in his fifty years; it would have the final word on Jack Davies. He hadn't bargained for such an epitaph.

He felt utterly alone.

*

As he walked into the clearing he could see the others had left. He felt the ashes of the fire. They were cold.

He hadn't encountered them in retracing his steps. They must have taken the other fork in the path as it exited the clearing. He struck off again in that direction.

It was late afternoon by the time Jack reached the others. No one said anything about his disappearance. It was as if he had never left.

\*

We moved on for a couple of days living off a few packets of biscuits and drinking rainwater from pools by the roadside. The A1062 took us in the direction of Danny's family home. Jenny was finding it tough going but not one of us ever thought of leaving her behind. I guess none of us wanted to leave this world with one more blight on our consciences; maybe it was the feeling that we could control nothing else in our lives so we might as well at least try to improve the odds of finding something better in the hereafter.

The days were drawing in and the air becoming colder. We had no way of telling but guessed it must be late November or early December. Not that the months made any sense any longer; mother nature had long since stopped conforming to the calendar man had tried to impose.

An Easterly wind brought sharp gusts of icy air down across Western Europe and East Anglia from the Russian steppes. Jack would insist on us keeping up a steady pace and walking six hours a day, but we covered less and less ground as the days went by. Then, one morning we woke to find the world white with snow, flakes falling the size of the palms of your hand and blanketing the iron brown fields. We broke camp and continued following the road as best we could. The snow fell steadily all day throwing a virgin blanket over the landscape, drifting and rubbing out the boundary between road and hedge and field with only the occasional prints of foxes and birds to break the smooth surface ahead. Looking behind at our footprints in the snow it was easy to believe we were the first and the last souls ever to wander this earth and that it wouldn't take long for the falling snow to cover all trace of where we'd been.

Josh started to complain of headaches and feeling a chill. We gave him our scarf, balaclava and gloves. Late one afternoon, as dusk fell, we turned into a deserted farmhouse.

We could see only by the eerie after-light which

snow seems to store like a battery and leak out at dusk. A tractor and the great hulk of a combine harvester stared out from a barn – great creatures now in permanent hibernation.

We found a dry wood store and got a fire blazing in the old inglenook. We sat Josh by the fireside and Jack persuaded him to take a couple of shots of whisky with a mug of black tea.

Jenny and Danny did the cooking. She would melt snowfall for drinking water and make up a vegetable stew from the piles of beet and swede in the barn. Sometimes Danny would go off foraging for food in the nearby woods. We didn't see what he brought back. We didn't want to. The stew was tasty and kept us going, whatever added ingredients he put in it.

The snow lasted for weeks. Each morning a new fall and drifting under the hand of the north easterly masked our footprints from the previous day. The drifting had reached the eaves at the back of the barn and the old timbers creaked with the weight when the wind blew full on that elevation.

The nights were basked with an eerie light as the moonlight bounced off the crystalline eiderdown that covered the buildings and fields around us. And the world was silent. More silent than I ever remember it before. Sitting still you could hear the blood in your arteries and something else. A thick viscous silence that seemed to emanate from every object. It was as if we were hearing the very background radiation, which was the echo of the universe's birth, of its big bang.

During the day there would be some melting and we would hear the metronomic drip, drips from the gutters. Come night-time, the temperature would drop again and freeze icy fingers hanging from the gutters and the trees. The wind would play chimes as the trees icicle burdens rattled against each other and shattered.

Sometimes we would hear a dog howling in the distance or a barn owl would flap past like a large pillow on the wing, it's wing beat slow and confident.

No matter how high we built the fire Josh couldn't seem to stop shivering. And he had a raging thirst. We had to go outside and scoop up snow in our hands to fill an old iron pot and melt on the fire for extra drinking water.

We slept each night fully clothed, buried in our sleeping rolls in a semicircle around the fire. We kept as close together as we could. Jack and Danny took turns to add logs to the fire through the night. Sometime, maybe two or three hours before daylight, Josh let out an awful scream, shaking as if some devil had gotten hold of him and was throttling the very life out of him. Jack and I tried to calm him down but he just kept screaming "NO! NO! NO! Don't know whether you call it a nightmare or whether he was hallucinating – guess it amounts to the same when you're in it. Whatever Josh 'saw' scared the hell out of him that's for sure.

In the early morning Jack used some of our powdered soup packets to make a hot cup for each of us. Josh was having trouble sitting up so Jack held him by one arm behind his back with the other bringing the cup to his lips to help Josh drink. There was a tenderness in the way Jack held that boy.

We stayed in the farmhouse for a quite a few days, I can't remember exactly how long. And all the while the snow fell outside. We found more logs out in the barn and had plenty to keep the fire going continuously. Soup and biscuits kept body and soul together. And all the while Jack looked after Josh.

Danny was still anxious to carry on and look for his mother, but no one was going anywhere until Josh was well enough. As Danny put it: "We've come this far together I'd feel like I was missing a limb if I had to leave one of you behind."

I guess that's what it comes down to in the end.

You can argue until you're blue in the face about politics, religion, economics – have what you will – but you only have the right to be called human if you look out for others and if you need others. We might be at each other's throats a lot of the time but we don't do well alone. Even the wolf still needs to run with his pack. Maybe that's what is going to make sure something comes out of all this mess. Eventually the survivors are going to find each other and will stick together in groups. Someone will start organising things and soon enough people are going to be working together to build, gather, and grow – all the basic necessities of life. Maybe this time though, some generation down the track will call a halt to so-called progress before it gets out of control, before we get to killing each other in millions and exhausting the planet.

Gradually Josh got stronger. The hallucinations stopped and his temperature came down. We knew he was on the mend when he picked an argument with Jack over the excesses of capitalism and then grinned when Jack rose to the bait. Josh was back with us.

Then one morning we woke to find the snow had stopped falling and a thaw was setting in. For the first time in what seemed a hundred years the sky was blue without clouds as if all the days of snowfall had wrung it dry of every last drop of moisture. Streams of melt water started to run in every crease and crevasse of the land anxious to find lower ground and to swell with others into a flood.

Some nights the sky cleared to reveal a million, million pinpoints of light from planets, to stars, to galaxies, to nebulae, to novae and on and on, all the flora and fauna of the heavens speaking in a chatter of light across different ages. We looked up at a picture which was all of history combined into one pointillist canvas. Indifferent to the affairs of men, the wars, the succession of Kings and Queens, the births and deaths of our famous, our joys and our tragedies, these messengers of light had made their way at perfect speed to announce what the universe looked like a thousand, a billion and more years ago.

Danny's mother used to say: 'Look, can't you see God himself up there?' But all we could see was rock and fire and gas in elemental confusion and so alien to our flesh and blood. How could one beget another, when the world is made up 99.99% of emptiness and the rest is dust and rock – how could that be a birth place for human creativity, joy, sadness, love. You can't make hope from atoms – they are just fundamentally different things. And so why would a God interested in love, sin, redemption create a universe whose 'stuff' is so alien in nature to the 'stuff' of humanity?

And so I could easily convince myself that Mum's God was not there and there were no others like ourselves living around these distant points of light. The human race is a freak of nature and it is not our improbability that is the worry, it is our irrelevance. Yet however complete my logic I was left more alone than a soul can stand.

So tonight I look up at the stars. Is the feeling any different? Is it any more lonely to know that many of those earthly accidents of physics and biology have likely been exterminated in the floods, famines and diseases of the last months? Does the loss of a few billion souls make a real difference to the emptiness of this inorganic universe? And yes it seems the feeling is deeper, more profound, and less theoretical.

Now, with proof that mankind can be eclipsed so readily there is no hiding place for the lonely soul; no place of make believe where men and women are driven to create history, technology and the next generation to take on this work. No place where those distractions of ambition and purpose enable us to forget the essential meaninglessness of what surrounds and dwarfs us.

\*

One day Danny said he was going to get more firewood from the house and started to scrunch through the deep white. But within a few moments he stopped and shouted back in the direction of the barn. We followed his deep prints whilst he pointed a few yards to his right.

"Someone else has been here – and recently 'cos there's no snowfall on top of these 'ere footprints."

Starting from near the barn door and taking an elliptic path up to the house were a separate set of footprints to those Danny had just made.

"Very funny, Danny," Josh said. "We haven't seen a soul in weeks and now you discover a Yeti in Suffolk."

"I ain't claimin' it's no Yeti. Them Wellington boots is the same size as mine. I don't expect your Yeti wears boots. Maybe it's the owner of this place or someone looking for him."

"Or maybe a sleepwalking Danny," Josh grinned.

"I don't sleepwalk."

"Not sure how'd you know but there's one way to settle it – let's follow the tracks and see who's at the end of them," Josh said.

"And what if that someone is armed?"

"Take the pitchfork from the barn wall. That

should put the fear of God into man or Yeti," laughed Josh.

"You stay here. I'll follow the tracks," Danny said. "I don't want to have to look after you as well as dealing with whoever's been hanging about here."

Danny started off treading in the anonymous tracks to ease his way and reduce the noise of his footfall. In a few minutes he reached the threshold of the farm house, stopped, then went in.

All was quiet except the occasional soft thud of snow falling from the branches of the oaks growing at the edge of the field.

Beyond the farmhouse was a field bordered by fence and post. The run of fencing that was perpendicular to the farmhouse ran some two hundred yards down to a stream then turned through ninety degrees to go behind the big barn.

Moments later there was a banging and the figure of Danny emerged from behind the farmhouse and struck off following the line of the fencing.

"Must have come out the back door. Where's the fool heading now?" asked Josh.

We watched Danny's figure wade knee deep in snow along the line of the fence.

The cold was freezing our breath against the cobalt blue of the winter sky. Josh started to flap his arms to try to warm up. "I'm going back indoors. We've got a few sticks of firewood left. I'm not counting on Danny coming back with any more now he's decided to play the fool."

The fire was licking around the bits of kindling when we heard Danny banging hard on the small door to the rear right hand side of the barn.

"Come here, you two, look at this."

On opening the door we found a red-faced Danny, huffing and puffing with the exercise of walking through the deep snow and again pointing at tracks a few feet from where he was standing.

"Look, they finishes at the door. Whoever it was, walked a path from the front door of the barn through the farmhouse then back round the perimeter field round to this back door."

"But where is he now?" asked Jack.

"Standing right in front of you, having a good laugh inside I'll bet," Josh said.

"Come on Danny, own up now."

"I ain't been out before this morning, not once. Them tracks ain't mine," professed Danny.

"Well they're not mine and Jack's not claiming them either."

Josh tried his boot size inside one of the mystery footprints.

"Looks a pretty close fit to me," Danny said.

"And so was yours," Josh retorted. "This is like Cinderella."

"We aren't going to solve things that way. I think we all took the same big size 12 in Wellington boots from that shoe shop at the last mall – with the same tread pattern – which looks a lot like this one over here," he said pointing at the orphan tracks.

"So either our mystery man shops in the same places as us, or one of us is having a laugh," Josh said. "Come in anyway, you're letting the cold in. Maybe we can get the mystery man to go up to the house and get us some more firewood; this fire isn't going to see the hour out."

# CHAPTER 10

# JENNY

Jenny never seemed all that comfortable when we were all together. Maybe we were just too much for her; I don't know. David was OK; nothing seemed to fuss him much.

Sat around the fire one evening, Jenny asked: "How long have you been travelling... together?" We were silent for a few moments then Josh spoke: "I remember leaving London on the tube; well until we got to Stratford. Then it's a bit of a blank after that for a while. I found Jack first I think and, I guess, we must have picked up Danny later but I'm not sure exactly when. Strange, I don't really recall exactly how we came together. I guess when the world's upside down like this your memory plays tricks." Josh looked around for some kind of reassurance.

Danny spoke: "I don't rightly know where we met either. About the first thing I remember is seein' the bodies and hearing Jack and Josh arguin'."

Jack was silent. Jenny waited but he said nothing. She seemed to decide that was as much information as she was going to get on that subject and moved on: "Whatever happens, life's never going to be the same for any of us I guess. You are young enough to adapt and create a new life. I'm not sure if David and I can do that."

"Sometimes, I can see nothing but pain ahead," Jack said. "I've done my level best to stay positive and keep us moving on, setting a small target for the day – to reach the next village... to make shelter before dusk... but optimism is sometimes just too heavy a weight. There have been mornings when I just wanted to give up... to curl up into a ball and sign off. Danny's driven by wanting to find his mum and sister. Me? I don't know what keeps me going. Maybe it's just the journey 'cos I can't see anything at the end of it. I think Josh feels something the same."

Josh looked up for a few moments then his eyes fell to the fire.

David spoke: "I read a book on psychology once which talked about 'sub-personalities'. They are kind of parts of yourself, parts of your overall personality. Like you might have a particularly lazy streak or a stubborn or envious part. And we come into play in different circumstances or when some trigger stimulates us. The book said that an individual sub-personality can take you over if you have a particularly strong reaction to a situation."

"It's like Jekyll and Hyde?"

"Maybe, but people usually have many sub-personalities, not just two. But most of us are not really very aware of them in the sense of seeing them clearly as different facets of ourselves and knowing them when they appear. We might just be aware of a change of feeling or mood. Like Jack was saying… some days he feels some purpose and strides out and the part of him that likes to succeed, to win in life, is in the ascendancy and then… then, other days the pessimist gets the upper hand and he wants to give up.

"Well, the book went on to say that these parts of us are created in childhood and are drawn from the different aspects of our parents or carers. Whilst there are some common ones, we each have a differing set or mix of sub-personalities dependent upon the formative influences and people in our early lives.

"Sounds a bit like Mr. Men – the kid's books – you

know, Mr Nasty, Mr Naughty, Mr Smiley…" Danny said.

"Yeah… maybe children recognise this more easily than adults – they are less controlled and more readily trigger into one or other of their sub-personalities. Anyway, the book said that, for adults certainly, one of the tasks of life is to re-integrate these sub-personalities into a whole, to own them and be aware of them but not to be slaves to them. You know how uncomfortable the feeling of jealousy can be, eating you up and getting in the way of you feeling, thinking, doing other things. It can become obsessional. That's when you are in the 'grip' of a particular sub-personality, 'Mr Jealous' for want of a better name. To pull yourself out of this you have to recognise the sub-personality and see it for what it is – just a part of you which has become very active. If we can be aware that the sub-personality is at large, know it for what it is and know that it is not the whole of us, then we can manage the impact of that sub-personality.

"Staying in a particular sub-personality can distort our actions. Standing back and seeing that we have choices, we can invoke other more constructive sub-personalities and change our response.

"What's the bit of us that stands back then? Mr

Who?"

"I imagine it is as some kind of central, core person... an 'observer'... You know how there seems to be a bit of you which is a bit more detached and can look down on what's happening."

"Not sure he's been out much on this trip."

"Integration seems to be the key according to the psychologists. You don't disown any of the parts of you, even the nasty parts. To develop you accept the bad bits as well as the good, because they also do you a service in some way when they are present. For example, Mr Jealous may be a useful reminder that you deserve some of the good things in life too."

"What happens if you don't listen to the bad parts, you sort of suppress them?" Josh asked.

"We get more insistent and louder until they get some satisfaction. The risk is that they, you, blow a fuse instead of a more moderate response to some situation."

"Guess maybe we should all be on the lookout for our sub-personalities. Wonder which two of Jack and Josh's sub-personalities have been fighting with each other so much?" Danny asked.

*

Danny threw another stick on the fire then said: "I hoped I would find somebody special to be with; you know get married and bring up kids. Do all those ordinary things couples complain about. Don't know how that was goin' to happen, working all day and living with mum but can't see it 'appening now."

"What does that mean to you finding someone special like that?" Jenny asked.

Danny looked sheepish. "Well I wants the usual hugs 'n kisses like that, it's someone who knows me, who knows how I am, kind of understands what it's like to be Danny and cares what happens to him. Course my mum knows me in a way and she cares... but it's different; family is one thing, a wife is something different. They are separate people not mixed up with you in the way family is. They can see you more clearly, I think and they don't have to love you like family do; they chooses to. You could say it means more when someone picks you out like that; picks you out from the crowd as the one they want to be with. With families it's automatic like, you're born into them. I want to be chosen."

Jack spoke next: "It's a fine thing to find someone special. Not something I was blessed with. Maybe that's something I regret about the future too; but it takes two to make a couple and I've been missing 'lost in action' most of my life. I wasn't there to keep my end of the bargain, truth be told. But the thing I'll miss most is the next generation. My sons are full-grown, doing their own thing; don't see much of them now. I'd hoped I might see their children, have a hand in their upbringing. I guess I made plenty of mistakes bringing up my own. But they say you learn most from your mistakes, so I should make an A-star granddad." He laughed a small, uncertain laugh and wiped his cheek.

"Do you know where your sons are?"

"One lives in the USA and the other in Australia. About as far away as they could manage to get. I hope they're not living through the kind of mess we've got here right now. We speak every month or so but I, I don't know where or how they are right now.

"There's another reason I'd like to have had grandchildren. I don't remember much of my childhood before the age of, say, eleven. There are big gaps. Maybe things will come back when I'm older but being a grandfather kind of offered a way of living through the Tom Sawyer days vicariously and painting in a part of the canvas that has been blank.

"I do remember a time when I was about six years

old. I remember it because it was that summer that my auntie Jessie died. I had to go to the funeral in a big dark church and say prayers from the book with my parents. Everyone was dressed up and had long faces. A lot of the women were crying and blowing their noses in handkerchiefs. The men just looked stern. The men always seemed to look stern then. They said at school there was a 'recession' and lots of men were losing their jobs in and around South Kirby. Even worse the mines were shutting down and there was nothing much for the men to do. My father still had work; he ran a funeral parlour. Folks would laugh and say he would be the last one to go out of business. Dad didn't laugh much; I guess I can kind of understand why. Anyway he worked long hours and would often go back to the offices in the evening to finish paperwork or plan the next day's work. He often said 'we should never forget how lucky we are; things in life can change in just a toss of a coin. Look at those lads in the dole queue.' He would tell Mum off for spending on things like ornaments for the house.

"One day when I got home from school I heard Mum talking to someone in the living room. As I got through the door I saw the back of a man's head sat in Dad's armchair, a balding head, not my Dad's. 'Jack, love, say hello to Mr Goodyear. Mr Goodyear is going to be staying with us for a while.' A tall, dark moustached man rose from the chair and turned to me. I remember shaking his hand; it was soft and a little damp, not like the men who usually came to our house who would squeeze your hand so hard as if to crush it.

"Mr Goodyear was given the room at the top of the house, the converted attic. We had a big old house left to us by my dad's parents when they died. Dad said it cost a lot to heat. There were coal fires in the bedrooms but we hardly ever lit them. Extra blankets and hot water bottles were pulled out of cupboards when winter came. Except Mr Goodyear did light his fire. Dad always saw to it that he had plenty of coal to burn. 'He's a paying guest so he's entitled' Dad would say. Mr Goodyear was a lodger. He worked as an Insurance salesman for the Co-op during the day and kept himself mostly to himself during the evenings. He didn't go out much and never brought anyone back to the house. Mum would make dinner for him but he would usually eat alone, after we had finished our meal. It wasn't that he was unfriendly, just seemed to like to keep separate and that became the routine. The thing I remember most though was Mr Goodyear's stamp collection. He had ten maybe a dozen big albums full of stamps from all over the world. From time to time he would offer to show me parts of the collection. Dad told me I wasn't to ask as I wasn't to bother Mr Goodyear. But when he asked me that was alright. We'd open up one of the albums on the kitchen table and he would tell me about the stamps where they came from, where he had got them, how rare or common they were. Sometimes there were what he called misprints where there was some mistake made in printing and because they were different and there would be so few of them then those stamps were more valuable. It seemed to me then that there weren't many other parts of life where a mistake made something more valuable.

"Mr Goodyear said that his job was secure but it didn't pay much. A bit like Dad's. So he couldn't afford expensive holidays abroad. Collecting stamps was a way of travelling without the expense and without needing days and weeks off work. For him the stamps were a window onto a world he was never going to see for real. A window he could look through from his own bedroom in Yorkshire. He could visit places as far flung as Papua New Guinea, Colombia, Korea, Zambia, Tanganyika and Nyasaland, Gold Coast... I remember the birds and animals in so many different, rich colours; colours you would never see in Yorkshire unless it was through one of those kaleidoscopes we used to get as children on trips to the seaside. And then there would be the heads of rulers: kings, presidents, generals – they looked foreign, mysterious somehow and yet you thought that any moment they might start speaking to you from the face of the stamp. Mr Goodyear had an atlas and whenever we looked at a new section he would point out the country in the atlas and that would make the journey more real. He seemed to know a lot about each of the countries-the population, the languages spoken, who was in charge, the main crops or industries, who we had been at war with. He was one of the most travelled people I have ever met. Sometimes if Mum was busy in the kitchen I was allowed to go up to Mr Goodyear's room. He would have a toasting hot fire going in the cold months and we would huddle up in the armchair that my dad had put up there for him and do a 'round the world' trip in an evening.

"It's funny I don't remember much else about him. I suppose the stamps are what caught my imagination and there wasn't much else to remember. He left quite suddenly one day. The night before he left, I was in bed and I heard Mum and Dad shouting downstairs. It was unusual for them to have a row. Mostly they didn't speak much except about practical things that needed to be done around the house. I don't suppose Dad's work was the kind of thing you talked about much and Mum was at home most for the day. But that night they were shouting, and both upset. I heard some snippets: 'you tell me how we are going to make ends meet', Dad was shouting; 'he can't stay', Mum kept screaming back at him.

"Anyway the next day Mum just said, 'Mr Goodyear is leaving us; he is moving out of the area.' And that was it. I didn't even get to say goodbye as he had gone when I got home from school. Although I didn't have any stamp album I would still visit those faraway places in my mind as I waited for sleep at night."

"And that little boy ended up in a very demanding job in the City – a big leap eh?" Jenny observed.

"I think my job has had enough of me now, and I have had enough of it, truth be told. The institutions we built fell apart when put under stress. They were based on a misunderstanding of what human wealth is. I spent so much time following the yellow brick road to the Far East, to India, Brazil, the US, in search of value that I missed what was under my nose," Jack said.

"You hear these bitter-sweet regrets from old guys or drunks and, of course, you think, 'no way I'm going to end up like that'; then one day you have one drink too many in a bar somewhere and someone is willing to listen and out it comes, all the pent-up, existential angst you have unconsciously suppressed, kept at bay. And you listen to yourself, disbelieving: this is not me, but you just keep on jabbering, spilling it out.

"I guess it's a kind of narcissistic pride but you just want to make a mark don't you; don't we all want to be immortal, in some way, at least to get a paragraph in some history book. I don't pretend it's about doing good works, leaving something to the next generation. We're selfish about this 'making a mark' thing. We want to avoid being extinguished, leaving no trace. It's like... if the day ends and is replaced by night then there was no point in the day ever having happened; there needs to be some remainder of the day or there was no purpose in it."

"Does any of this make sense," Jack asked, suddenly becoming self-conscious.

"Don't imagine you are alone in feeling like this," David said.

"I'd like to have kids too," Danny piped. "Wouldn't that be leaving your mark on the world? They carry a part of you into the future don't they? You had sons Jack, isn't that how it is?"

Jack thought for a few moments. "Sort of. I think it might feel more acute if you don't have kids. But they don't fill the hole completely. Yes, they carry on after you've gone and, hopefully, there are generations after that; but it's not you. As my sons got older, I realised they couldn't and wouldn't carry the burden of my unfulfilled hopes. They wouldn't do all the things I'd missed and most of all, they couldn't be me. They have our own fates and it's not to be my representative on earth. I'd like to think I'll stick around a bit longer in their memories; but I'm not even sure of that."

"There's something else," Jack continued after a few seconds. "I've lost something else; me. I've lost me. It's like I've been hollowed out. I'm here talking to you folks but I'm not really here. It's as if all the things that defined me, all the map co-ordinates that pointed towards Jack Davies have been swept away.

"A person has an identity because he's cut out like with a cookie-cutter from the background of life. He has shape because of all the other things around him, all the people he knows, the things he does, and the roles he plays. Where are all those things now? Where are the people, the place in the world that gave me shape? A person with an identity is 'the father of', 'an employee of', he's a borrower or a lender or a pensioner; he's 'the neighbour of', 'next door to'. How am I to find my bearings in this world now?"

"We have memories," Jenny said.

"Is that enough? Without them I can see it's even harder to define a person or even to have a sense of there being something… something that goes on, persists from moment to moment. But are they enough? I don't know. I remember things from back before the flood and, yes, that paints in the outline of Jack Davies a bit. But will it last? There are gaps; things or times I can't remember. My childhood; between six and eleven, is a bit of a blank; just an empty time when I can't find Jack Davies. I must have been somewhere. With my parents I guess; but I can't remember stuff. Did I just blink out of existence then and come back when I started secondary school, when all those other kids and teachers painted me in again? Memory's not a reliable thing. I'd hate to have 'me' dependent on memory."

"We are here now," Jenny said. "Can you get your bearings from us?"

Jack looked at the fire.

"Maybe. For the time being. But it seems… weak, fragile. Like I'm hanging by a thread. It's worse at night. What's left of the world disappears into darkness and I'm left only with what's in my head."

Josh hadn't heard Jack talk like this before.

"So, even before the floods I didn't have much of an answer to the 'why' question, but at least then I thought I had a handle on the 'who' and 'what'. I had some identity and purpose and could divert myself with work and make believe all that 'sound and fury' signified something. But now…" Jack tailed off.

Josh was sat in a lotus position, his narrow wrists and long-fingered hands draped across his legs palms up to the sky as if in a meditation pose. Every few minutes he took to playing with the frayed bottoms of his jeans… pulling out loose threads. His black hair, greasy and matted, was starting to fall over his shoulders. Between the frame of his hair and his beard a sharp, aquiline nose jutted out and two doe eyes of dark green looked at Jenny as she spoke.

"Before all this we had a position in society," Jenny continued. "Oh, that sounds a bit snobbish doesn't it… but I don't mean it like that."

"Well I suppose we had status… but we had something more. We had stability, predictability in our lives. Things worked, after a fashion; we went to the shop and there was food on the shelves; we turned a switch and a light came on. We saw people every day, people like us with the same kinds of hopes and fears. Things were just, well, normal — we had a society that worked okay. I know not everything in the garden was roses, but I ask you — has it ever been. Seems to me that the human race just has to have a certain amount of hardship and conflict; can't get by without it somehow. But society is a protection against the worst of this. That's why we huddle together isn't it, to stay warm and to be a sort of insurance policy for each other?"

"And that's all gone now," said Jack.

"I think we were losing it before the big sea hit. But now, well I just can't see any way back. I guess I was the space or shape made by everybody else's memories of me, relationships with me, expectations of me, hopes for me, wants from me — the things we liked about me, disliked, said to me, heard from me. What I'm saying is that if a person doesn't have all these other people then what is that person. Don't we just become shapeless, empty nothings?"

"You're my wife," David said. "Does that help?"

"Yes love, it does. We share memories; we've done a lot together. I can find a lot of me through what I've said and done with you. But…"

"But what?"

"But I don't think one can take one's whole existence and form from just one other person."

Josh had been rocking silently throughout Jenny's soliloquy.

"Maybe there's something in what you say. I know that after months on the streets I was losing a sense of me. I was becoming something different – a collection of a few basic human feelings – hunger, fear. Mostly I was shut down. How can somebody living in a cardboard box feel compassion? I could feel envy for sure.

"So 'I' had less and less content. The others used to walk past as if I wasn't there. That's a really good way of making somebody feel they have no place in the world. We didn't use our real names amongst the people sleeping under the arches; don't know why but we'd call each other Shorty or Ginger, or Dungarees. It was like we had no interest in our real names because everything was temporary anyway. Who needs a permanent label for something you're going to discard any minute?

"But somehow you made each other by your nicknames. What I fear now is there will be nobody left to do that. Our families are scattered… if they are alive. God knows what beach we will be thrown up on and whether we will ever find them again. Who then will give testament to who we were, that we were? We saw a Churchyard on our way here. It was maybe three feet deep in water and rising. The tombstones seemed almost to be stretching up, gasping for air, and trying to save history from simply being drowned."

A few minutes passed in silence then Josh cleared his throat: "For me the biggest loss would be having reached an end without ever having really started. I listen to what these two guys say and realise I've been avoiding the question."

"What do you mean?" David asked.

"Well, you'd think that someone who had rejected all the things others filled their lives with would walk slap bang into the problem of 'what's life for' pretty early on wouldn't you? But it seems like I rejected that too; or maybe because I haven't made such an investment in a career or family or anything else for that matter then I've avoided the rude awakening so far. Looking back I realise I was opting out as early as my schooldays. It seemed the only weapon I had to prove a point to my parents.

"I was thirteen when my parents packed me off to boarding school in Gloucestershire. 'It's not far and we can visit you often during term-time, and of course you'll come home during vacations. You'll enjoy being with the other boys –much less boring than being at home with us I'm sure.' Mum kept trying to reassure me all the way down the M4 in the car as Dad drove in silence. She didn't realise that I was more angry than anxious. Angry that they were packing me off like that. Of course I didn't know what I was going to find at this school, whether I would fit in; but that wasn't what was spinning round in my head right then. No it was: 'How dare they? How dare they bundle me up in the back seat and rush me down the motorway as if they were taking some trash to the public dump. It was all for their convenience, so my high-powered judge of a father could park his son while he gets on with his career and so my fragile mother could 'cope' with life without the daily worries of parenting. I wasn't able to say all that in those words at the time – it was more a mess of jumbled feelings but it's clearer now.

"I don't really know why I hated them so much for sending me away. Lots of boys from professional parents went to boarding school so why should I be different. I think it was Mum I was most angry with. Dad was just who he was and didn't pretend to be much interested in me or anything outside his work, but Mum did pretend, probably because that was the 'done thing'. What kind of mother would be disinterested in her offspring? No that wouldn't do. So she kept up a facade: 'We're so proud of Josh getting into one of the best private schools in the country. It gives him the best chance to get to Oxbridge later on... the school has a great record of turning out high grades; I guess we all want to give our kids the best chance in life don't we?'

"For me to settle in and enjoy the place would just have been too big an endorsement of my parent's decision to send me there, and I wasn't of a mind to prove them right. The schoolmasters were friendly at first encouraging me to get involved in school activities but the more I opted out then the more they got on my case about my academic progress. It's not that I was the bottom of the class – I was usually somewhere in the middle just on native wit without doing much work but that wasn't good enough. They decided I wasn't pulling my weight and that was a cardinal sin at Forest School. Driven by league tables of examination results they pushed every pupil to get the maximum out of them. So, within a couple of terms of arriving, the steady stream of end of term reports saying, 'disappointing performance' and 'could do so much better... pulling up socks time' started and the pattern persisted throughout my time at the school.

"My father was from a long line on his fathers' side of men who had risen to high positions in the English Judiciary. The law was 'in our DNA' he said. He clung to the hereditary theory of academic achievement and career choice for many years against the evidence of my accomplishments, or lack of, at school.

"Most vacations started and finished with Dad trying to give me a pep talk. If I wanted the good things in life I needed to 'knuckle down and work'. I was 'lucky to be given such an opportunity and shouldn't waste it'; 'I am making a big investment in you – look at the size of the school fees – and I want to see a return'. He tried bullying, threats, reproach, logic, moral blackmail but still the school reports bemoaned my waste of talent. Mum tried the emotional appeal but, though she never accepted it, she had long lost the emotional high ground with me. Dad hired personal tutors to give me intensive tuition before exams. Most of them left the house shaking their heads in frustration. But still I managed to keep my head just above water and got an 'acceptable' crop of GCSEs and then A levels – acceptable at least to me and to the school who could not find enough in my academic shortcomings or general opting out of school life to force the issue and to forsake my father's annual cheque by asking me to leave.

"I saw father's energy and belief slowly drain away as he attended meetings with my year tutor and the headmaster to discuss my progress. Some part of me took pleasure in his despair. I was dragged into most of the meetings which went round and round in circles as the school and my father scratched their combined heads as to what to do with Stieglitz junior, extracted reluctant undertakings from me that I would try harder next term and then, next time, discussed what had gone wrong. My father often came close to pinning the blame on the school-after all weren't they supposed to motivate as well as to educate the young men in our charge? Yet he never quite bearded the headmaster on this – fearing perhaps that that would be the last straw and that the school would elect to terminate my education as the fees were insufficient compensation for my dragging down the year's grade averages and being a damper on the mandatory *esprit de corps*. In any case he was never one to let me off the hook of what he saw as my responsibility.

"The pep talks became less frequent and less impassioned as he sensed that his words were just disappearing like stones down the bottom less pit of my intransigence – and he could hear no splash at the bottom.

"I didn't really make any close friends all the time I was at the school. There were a handful of guys I used to hang out with at break-time; some of the masters referred to us as the 'cynics society' because we scorned most of the schools extra-curricular activities, avoided the sports field like the plague and generally clustered around the mediocre in class grades. I did play handball at break times. There was a group of boys, including some of the cynics, who used to play against the gable end wall of the sports hall. There were official 'fives' courts behind the tennis courts at the school but we weren't having any of them. Beating the ball up against the side of the sports hall seemed, somehow, to symbolise our jealously guarded status as 'outsiders'.

"Once, in the first year, I came close to giving the school the excuse they later craved to send me down when I got into a fight in the schoolyard. I don't remember exactly what it was about, but one of the boys in the next year took a dislike to me and was poking fun. I just lashed out at him. I caught him square on the jaw and he went over. Within minutes there were fifty to a hundred adolescent boys gathered around, baying for blood, as the other guy got to his feet and proceeded to give me a good pasting until two of the masters arrived to break up the fray. We were both hauled up in front of the headmaster but I must have shown just sufficient contrition to avoid suspension and the inevitable inquests from my parents. The withdrawal of privileges like exclusion from the common room and its pool table and dartboard just pushed me further away from the mainstream.

"By the time 'A' level exams came around I think father had pretty much given up on me. He kept up the polite enquiries as to how I was doing on the few occasions we were at home together in the vacations, but the question was asked with an air of resignation. It had long since become clear I would not be following the well-trodden family path to the law – at least not to the right side of it. Parental aspiration had given way to anxiety – would I be able to get a job and live an independent life. I went through the motions of applying to university, largely because I couldn't think what else I would do and that at least was 'normal'. When I got the grades needed to go on and study history I experienced a small 'rally' in confidence, but of course it didn't last.'

"Anyway, answering Jenny's question what would

I fear the loss of most – the answer is: pretty much everything, everything I scorned before the floods came.

"It's ironic. When I was surrounded by the things men usually crave in life; when we were within touching distance, then I managed to convince myself I wanted none of it. Now the water has swept those things away, I'm having trouble maintaining my indifference."

"You're young still," Jack said. "Regret is something it takes years to earn."

The group sat quietly watching the dying flames of the campfire.

As the embers grew blood red and then breathed in and out with the breeze, Danny spoke: "I bin a thinking about what Jenny said; 'bout those sub-personalities. I kind of get what she means in some ways. Sometimes I surprises meself, like when I get angry and I'm not sure why. Well it's like somethin's been a goin' on behind a screen and it suddenly jumps out without warnin' like. Like Mr Angry has been there hidden all along and suddenly he just can't stay quiet any longer. It happens to Mum too. She'd be goin' about her business in the kitchen, ironin' or such like and then out of the blue she'd burst into tears. Her 'Mrs Sad' I s'pose just jumpin' out from behind the bushes. It'd take her as much by surprise as t'would me.

"Sometimes I seems to lose myself. Time seems to go by but I'm not there or at least I doesn't notice anything. It's like I've taken a timeout as they do in them American basketball games on TV. I'm there on the bench but not in the game at all. I've wondered if it's the same me on the bench as I is when I'm playin' the game. And when I've lost time like that and I come back who's to say it's the same Danny that comes back? We are all changing all the time aren't we? So maybe there's a string of we's like pearls on a necklace, not just one that goes on but a new one every minute, every second. Makes my head hurt."

"You're making mine hurt too," Jack said. "How come a gardener dwells on this kind of stuff?"

"You 'as to think o' something all day long; 'specially when you might not see another soul from dawn to dusk like when I'm working on some toff's big estate. Big estate like I'm guessin' you might 'ave Jack…"

"Memories," snorted Josh.

"What?"

"Memories. That's what makes you Danny, the

same bloke, from day to day. You have the same memories every morning you wake up and they are yours not somebody else's. In fact it doesn't even make sense to talk about having someone else's memories. You can have somebody else's shoes, or their wife, hah. But not their memories. Memories are very personal things and a big part of what makes us different from each other."

"He's got a point," Jack said.

Danny was quiet for a full minute.

"But we can both remember the same things and still be different people."

"Yes. But our memories can't be completely the same, experienced from the same position, identical sets of memories. If they were then we would have lived the same lives, then surely we would be the same person wouldn't we?"

Danny's brow furrowed as deep as a Suffolk field after the harvest.

"But my memories change with time; I get new ones, forget old ones; my granddad is eighty-one and can't but remember his own name, bless 'im. Does that mean he's stopped... well... stopped being anybody 'cos he can't remember nothin'?"

"I don't know. His body is still there, but then I guess you are going to say that's changed a lot over the years too. It seems to me the nearest we can get to defining a person is that we have much the same memories, and much the same bodies from day to day and though we change a bit at a time, it's gradual. Like a tree growing from an acorn to a sapling into a big oak – the changes are so gradual we can still call it the same tree.

"Well if we need our bodies to be us then there really isn't anybody to carry on when we die… If you see what I mean."

"Guess not. Guess that's about the sum of it. Whatever we are, I can't see that we can be anything but a pile of ashes when we go and you can't keep memories in a jar of ashes now can you?"

"Sure seems a lonely kind of world. We're not sure about each other and we're not even sure about ourselves. But if we really felt that way then why would we fight so hard to stay alive?"

"I don't know about you but I'm pretty convinced I exist. This fucking knee is killing me. Don't tell me this is just an illusion or a pain dangling in mid-air. No, there's a me for sure and it's me that has this throbbing feeling. And I'm unique!"

"The same can hardly be said for you two. You haven't got my pain as proof you exist. All I see is two bodies making movements and sounds. For all I know you are just the most advanced form of robot."

"There's gratitude. You dig a guy out of a hole and the next thing you know, you are a piece of make believe, a tin man without a heart. Bring on the *Wizard of Oz* why don't you, since you're the only superior, feeling life form amongst us."

"No offence meant."

"It's just that, well… I don't know about this stuff; it's a mystery."

"But not one we have to figure out today anyway," Danny said.

We all slept fitfully that night. Conversations whirling round in our head.

# CHAPTER 11

## CROSSING OVER

The weather had changed again for the worse. Rain fell in sheets with the wind rasping against the sides of our faces. Sudden gusts grabbed our clothing with steel fingers tugging and ripping, pulling, tearing. The air was waterfall thick.

We took turns in helping Jenny to walk, her left arm clinging to our shoulder, the walking stick in her right hand, feeling out in front of her. We could see only a few yards ahead; the world beyond had simply dissolved and washed away.

The ground beneath our feet turned to mud betraying our every step as we slithered and slid our endless way around the hillside. Every twenty yards we stopped and waited for Jenny to catch her breath, then pushed on again into the torrential gloom, testing the ground as if it were littered with landmines.

"How much further; I can't go on much further," Jenny screamed into David's ear, her words ripped apart and scattered by a dismembering wind.

"We have to cross the bridge. The river is swollen to breaking point. This may be the only chance we have to cross. Hold on now; hold on we'll get you over…"

David's voice was stretched like a violin wire, ready to snap at one more turn.

As we rounded a rocky outcrop a fork of lightning lit up the scene below our feet. Fifty feet down, the valley boiled with seething waters as the river tossed and somersaulted, all flailing limbs and open mouth, ricocheting off the valley sides then writhing, falling, bouncing, lunging down, down, down.

A worn limestone path led down from the rocks helter-skeltering to an old stone footbridge across the river.

"We have to make the bridge; it's the only way," Jack shouted above the storm.

We stumbled like new-borns, unsure of our feet, down the path. The limestone reflected what little light there was to show our way. The raw power of the river seemed to grow with each step nearer as its booming merged with the thunder to fill the air with drums.

Another fork of lightning and the bridge flickered in and out of existence. Through the staves of rain we could see half the bridge had gone and the river was eating away at the path either side as if to rip away its moorings.

We reached the beginning of the bridge and froze.

"Come on. Come on. It's going to collapse. We have to go now."

Jack was holding Jenny now and urging her on. There was room only for maybe two people abreast to pass over what remained of the old stone arch of the bridge.

"Go on. Go on you guys. Be ready to grab us," Jack shouted.

In turn, the human tightrope-walked the arch as the river pushed and tugged at the old stone joints, spray shooting fifteen feet in the air.

"Come on; I've got you," Jack shouted, his cheek against Jenny's. He moved crablike across the arch, first his left leg sliding out across the stones, then bringing his right to meet it. His left hand waving for balance and his right shoulder still firmly under

Jenny's arm.

We were half way across when the wall of water hit.

The cold squeezed the air from Jack's lungs as he tumbled through the rushing, foaming waters. Within the moment we were hit, Jenny was ripped away from him. All was raging blackness. The current grabbed his limbs and flung him around like a child's rag doll on a tossing, flailing, circling, plunging carousel ride. Desperate lungs burning, he pulled at the water reaching for the faint shimmer of light above, then pulled again, his head bursting, screaming you have to let go, when suddenly he broke the surface and sucked, sucked like great empty bellows to fill his chest. For seconds things went black again as the air filling his lungs started the journey to his brain.

'Aaagh!' He let out a roar as his shoulder hit something, a rock, just under the water's surface.

From the bank we could see Jack's black hair bobbing up and down, a hundred yards downstream and rushing away from them. Jenny had disappeared when the water hit. We didn't see her resurface.

We were running now along a worn path at the top of the riverbank, keeping our eyes on Jack's head, bobbing like an apple.

"Jack, Jack, grab onto something, we're here," shouted Josh.

Jack's body suddenly jerked and his head swivelled to face upstream towards the two. Josh was close enough now to see Jack's eyes wide, dark pupiled, staring; not with fear but with what looked like resignation.

"Jack!"

Fifty feet ahead was a group of rocks jutting out of the swirling waters.

"Jenny! Jenny!" David screamed in desperation.

"Jenny!" His eyes searched the boiling river surface looking for any sign of her blue jacket or silver hair. Nothing.

Jack seemed to pirouette in the water, arms flailing, scooping trying to manoeuvre himself in the direction of the rocks. Josh was ahead of him now and looked around the riverbank. To his left the floods had thrown up a thick tree branch. He grabbed hold and pulled one end, the other gouging a deep furrow in the mud. In a few moments he reached the waterline and saw Jack jammed by the current up against the group of rocks.

"Catch hold, Jack, catch hold," he shouted feeding the length of the branch out between the rocks.

Jack had both arms wrapped around the rock, unwilling to risk letting go.

"Catch hold; come on man you've got to…"

At that moment hauling his travelling companion back to land meant something to Josh, meant more than anything he could remember for a long time.

Jack's head turned to look in Josh's direction. Seconds later his right arm inscribed a circle in the air seeking the tree branch whilst he hung onto the rock with his left. He waved around blindly for a few moments then connected with the branch and gripped hard around the reassuring bark. After a moment more of doubt or indecision he let go of the rock and flung out his left hand to grab the branch again. "Hold on; we'll get you in. Just hold on for Christ's sake!" shouted Josh.

By this time Danny was alongside Josh helping pull on the branch to land our catch. Seconds later Jack lay on his side spewing water and gasping for breath on the riverbank.

"Where's David?" asked Josh.

"He ran on further, trying to find Jenny. We couldn't see nothin'; I don't know where she is," Danny replied.

*

We scoured the riverbank all night and into the next day. There was no sign of Jenny. David would not give up; he kept going for hours on end, searching the banks, wading into the shoals to search amongst the rocks. None of us found it in themselves to tell him to give up. How can you give up? It was clear he never would.

The storm abated on the second day. For three nights we camped without firelight on higher ground fifty yards or so from the river. There was a three-quarter moon suffusing the valley with an ethereal light. Though exhausted, sleep was fitful. Each night we would hear the sound of David moving around outside then his footfall disappearing in the direction of the river.

There were no rations left and we were down to the last two litre bottles of water. The river was still an angry brown flood. We would drink from it only when there was no other choice.

"David, we can't stay any longer." Jack was the first to say it.

"We need to find new supplies, otherwise we are going to die here. I'm sorry David, but she's lost; you know that don't you. She would want you to leave now, look after yourself."

"You go," was David's response. "I'm staying; going to keep on down river; she could have fetched up anywhere. I'm not leaving her. It's okay; you go. There's no reason for you to stay."

"David, come with us. She's lost."

"Come where? Do what? You don't get it do you?" David was becoming exasperated with our pleadings.

"Don't you remember how you answered Jenny's question?" he continued. "The thing you would miss is family, someone to love. Well I have that in Jenny and I'm not about to give up on it. I'm going to keep looking."

An hour later we pulled our rucksacks over our shoulders and said our goodbyes to David.

We set off east, Danny in the lead. He seemed to recognise the outcrops of land peering above the water's surface but didn't say anything. None of us did. It was a relief just to be able to follow him without question.

We had no idea of time. It was like we'd been walking all our lives, together. How long ago was it that we left London? We were different people then, weren't we? It was a hundred years ago.

Everything we once were had been washed away. Somewhere out there in these floodwaters were the fragments of our old selves; shattered pieces of memory floating, separated from each other. Occasionally two pieces came together like a jigsaw puzzle and then were ripped apart again by the shifting waters.

Jack and Josh had another spat. There was still some tension between them but it seemed weaker now. Josh had used the can opener at the last overnight camp. Now he couldn't find it. He said he'd never had it. Didn't seem like he was lying; he just didn't remember using it. The denial irritated the hell out of Jack. "You live in your own little world," he'd shouted. Josh got defensive again. I guess remembering things is really important to who we are and so someone putting doubt on our memory is like a personal attack.

# CHAPTER 12

## COMING HOME

We were getting closer now. Danny recognised the rolling hills and copses surrounding the villages near his home. He led the way. Each mile we covered he seemed to get more and more agitated... anxious.

Eventually, we reached the brow of a hill and looked down onto a valley. "There's the house, that's it," Danny said.

In the valley floor was what looked like an old farmhouse, near a river still swollen with the rains. Danny started running. We had our work cut out trying to keep up with him. He went faster as he got near the house until, suddenly, he stopped about thirty yards from the fence.

"What's wrong?" Josh asked. "Let's go up and see if there's anybody around."

Danny just stared at the front door.

Around us was a real mess; uprooted trees and branches; a shed, maybe for keeping chickens in or something, on its side flattened like a cardboard box; the yard to the house littered with old sacks, a rake, boots, like the barn had just spewed out everything inside it.

"Been hit by the flooding; water's subsided now. Look, you can see where the water got to," Jack said pointing at the stain running along the ochre painted walls about a metre above ground level. Suddenly Danny ran headlong towards the door and bashed it open with his shoulder shouting, crying 'Mum, Mum.'

When we got inside we heard him running around from room to room upstairs still shouting, shouting all the while. It stank in there. There were still stagnant pools of water hanging around on the stone kitchen floor; the carpets in the other rooms were rotting. It didn't look like anybody had been there for months, maybe more. The flies were disgusting; filling the air with their fat sound. Danny stopped shouting. A few seconds later we just heard a long, high-pitched howling, like some wounded animal. When we found him he was sat knees pulled up under his chin in a corner of one of the bedrooms. The bed was unmade, a duvet half on the floor had soaked up the damp from the air like blotting paper and hung there covered in mould. Against one wall was an old wardrobe, it's drawers hanging open and sagging as the wood had swollen and split, joints breaking open under its own weight.

It took maybe half an hour or more for Danny's howling to die down and longer still before he could talk.

Josh tried to console him. "She'll have found her way out to higher ground Danny. There'll have been neighbours to help I'm sure and, anyway, it sounds like your mum was the resourceful type. She'll have made her way. If not, we'd find... Well we'd know. There's no sign anyone's about or even been about here for some time."

"He's right," Jack chipped in trying to inject some confidence into his voice.

"You changed your tune," Danny muttered.

"What do you mean?" asked Josh.

"You changed your tune. Early on you said she was dead; you said Mum was bound to be dead and I should just get used to the idea. How come you're changing your mind now then, when she's not here, not home like she's supposed to be? How come?"

Danny's voice was rising in anger.

"I never said that. I wouldn't have said that. How could I know anyway?"

"You and your university education; you seem to know everythin' and nothin'. You can't make your mind up about this can you? A little thing like whether somebody's alive or dead is just too much for your big brain ain't it?"

"I never said that. I wouldn't," Josh said again in a whisper this time as if talking to himself; trying to persuade himself.

Danny rocked to and fro again on his haunches then reached out to grab the side of the bedroom drawers and heaved himself upright.

He walked slowly out of the bedroom door and started down the stairs. Half way down he stopped and put his hand on the flower-pattered wallpaper, looking at it as if trying to remember something; something buried deep in the silt of days and weeks on the road; something just beyond the reach of his fingertips.

"We can't stay here," Jack said, back downstairs in the kitchen.

"I'm not leaving," Danny said.

"You... What are you going to do here Danny?

There's no food, no water. How long do you think you'll last? She's not here, son. We have to move on; we have to move on if we're going to stay alive and if we are going to have any chance of finding your mum."

"I'm not leavin' here. She'll come back if she's still alive. And if she's not… Well, what's the point?"

"What do you mean?"

"I mean there's no point. Not for me anyway. You can do what you want. But I can't see any point in movin'. We've been movin' for what seems a lifetime and where's that got us, eh? Things ain't getting' any better by movin'. Sides, I want to be here when she comes back. I ain't a full person without her and home. I can't seem to hold onto myself in all the mess out there. Like a boat with no anchor.

"The only thing that's kept me goin' is the thought of reachin' home. What else is there? Only this isn't how I imagined things. You remember places as they were when you were happy; not like this. I got to put things back together again, somehow. And I need my family around me to do that right. A man's only as much as the people who love him and the place he belongs. If you take away the two of those things we are empty and nothing we do or say adds up to anythin'.

"... had to learn to do things around the house from as early as I can remember. Dad wasn't very handy. Mum told me later that he was often out of it on the booze. So if she needed a plug changed or some shelves put up I was the one with the screwdriver. Maybe it was just me gettin' ready for later life when I'd have to make a livin' with me hands or it was just that we all knew that dad wouldn't stick around, so there was no use leanin' on him.

"Mum was very house-proud; liked to have everything in its place, spick 'n span. She'd Hoover the floors like she was trying to get out some stain that I could never see. The beds would be made without a wrinkle and my shirts would be ironed to the same smoothness; I was the best ironed lad in the school. But I'd feel the rough edge of her tongue if I left my muddy boots in the kitchen. Everything and everywhere in the house had to be neat and tidy in case somebody, anybody, dropped by. She was always a worrier; scared of life you might say. I think maybe that's why she needed to keep things under control. She'd worry about her job in the local factory, imagining she'd be the first to be laid off if times got tough. I never knew how likely that was, but I came to believe that if God himself had come down and swept away her troubles then, half an hour after he'd left, she would have piled up a whole heap of other things to worry about.

"She'd worry about my sister, Melanie, and she wouldn't hide her worries when she went on at Melanie in front of me: 'You mind what I told you about those boys' she'd say; 'they're only after one thing at this age; at any age come to think. A nice girl doesn't give it out just like that; she waits until she is old enough to know her feelings and to trust another's; until she's old enough to know the responsibility that's involved in bringing another soul into the world; old enough to feed another mouth well as her own.

"'I don't like you makin' yourself up to the eyeballs like that young lady. It's just an invitation of the worst kind. Mark my words, you dress like a slut and they'll treat you that way. I don't care if all the other girls are wearing the same, you're not them.'

"My sister was three years older than me and was cutting herself free from Mum's apron strings as fast as she could. We weren't close as brother and sister though she was never unkind to me. It was just that she had different interests and was dead set on breaking free from home. When she left school she got a job in an office as a secretary and it wasn't long before Mum told me that 'our Mel' had 'shacked up' with some bloke she'd met at work. About a year later she had a baby boy. She used to visit on Sundays, just her and the baby, and sometimes Mum would babysit during the week, but as the months and years went by we saw less of her. Mum spoke less about her until eventually it seemed like the waters had just closed over her and her name was never mentioned.

"I don't really remember Dad; guess I was too young when he left. It seems like a big gap really; a man should have a father – that's just how things are meant to be – and when you don't it kind of sets you apart in a bad way. People like teachers and other kids tend to ask questions about your family – like what do they do for a livin', what do they think about this or that. Of course you can just tell them outright that your dad left but that seems to start off all sorts of other questions, some of which they seem unsure about asking but you know the question is still there anyway, still there in their heads.

"I can't ever remember seein' her and him together like a man and wife showin' loving to each other. Not like our next-door neighbours Mr and Mrs Johnson; they were always laughin' with each other and holdin' hands and things like that. I often thought that was how I'd like to be one day, but wondered if I would know how.

"I didn't go out much of an evening. Especially, when Melanie had gone, Mum liked to have the company. Some of the boys at the local comprehensive school thought this was 'funny' and made jokes but I'd do my best to ignore them. As I got bigger they were a bit more careful about making fun of me so much 'cos I was about the size of two of them, with arms powerful enough to snap 'em in half. Our neighbours had said that I would have to 'be the man of the house' when Dad left. Later, they'd often ask Mum what she was feeding me that I got so big. I reckon the muscles and brains get shared out at birth and if you gets more than your share of one you get less of the other. So the world is made up from men who make their way by either bein' stronger or bein' smarter than others. It's not often you find both, or neither, in one man. In that way I guess there's a kind of fairness about things, I guess.

"It's pretty clear I was one of those that got the muscles rather than the grey cells. The lads at school weren't so clever either but there was a few of 'em thought they was better than me. They'd call me 'genius' and things like that. I didn't mind it so much in the class because there was only them 'n their kind to hear – except sometimes the girls would giggle at their stupid jokes. But waiting for the bus there'd be other folks around. Sometimes the old women in the village would say 'leave the poor lad alone', but that just made it worse, it was embarassin' to have everybody's eyes on me.

"Anyway when the day came to leave school I was kind of happy and sad at the same time. Happy to be away from those lads digging at me; but sad too… it seems strange, I know, but it was like I was leavin' something behind that I'd never be able to go back and get.

"I don't know if you two can understand what I'm sayin'. I couldn't have lived like the two of you. What do you have to hang onto? I've heard your stories and I'm…. Well, I'm sorry for you. No, that sounds too full of meself. I mean… I'm sad. I think I got a dose of sadness from the two of you. It's like you're carrying a sackful of regrets that you can't put down. And now the floods have come there's no way back. There's no way you can find the lives you used to live or the ones you wished you'd lived.

"Maybe we three are not so different though. Josh, opted out of being with people and, in a way, I guess I did somethin' similar working alone most of the time. Jack, I think, opted out of being with himself, keepin' busy makin' more money than he had time to count so he never had to talk to himself. I've come to know you a bit these past few days and weeks and you're more like brothers than you might care to say.

"Like brothers. Yeah, like you came from the same block of wood. The grain may be running in different directions but you're kind of different cuts from the same stuff.

"And brothers fight don't they? Wonder why that is? It's as if there's not enough space for two or more saplings in the same ground. Fightin' for the sun maybe. You two are like that. But somehow you need to fight. It's that what keeps you goin'. You might do it with clever arguments about money or the environment but those are just the weapons, the knives you use for the fight. And if you didn't have those you'd find something else is my guess. In fact if you hadn't met each other you'd have to invent each other and probably that's what you did before all this mess.

"Maybe brothers fight because we see our bad bits in the other. A brother can be a place where you put all the stuff you don't like about yourself, so you don't have to own up to it bein' your own. Maybe that's why you hate them and love them all at the same time. But I've got no brother. Ma had another boy after me but he died young. I never got to know him and he was too tiny ever to take on my bad bits. People say 'that there Danny he's a good lad'; says that all the time to Ma. But I don't know where I put the bad bits; must have gone somewhere 'cos I'm sure we all must have them, those dark bits."

Jack and Josh had been silent through Danny's soliloquy. Outside the light was failing. The wind bent the trees as dark clouds gathered to wash the earth again as if trying to rid it of a deep stain.

Josh broke the silence. "I think we should gather some stuff for a fire and bunk down here tonight. Let's decide what we do in the morning."

*

The next morning Danny still didn't want to leave his mother's house. Eventually the others persuaded him that the best chance of finding her was to press on to higher ground. We struck off due west.

It seemed like something had begun to change in those last few days. It started around the campfire with Jenny and David, I think, and got strengthened after Jenny was lost in the river. It was as if we saw each other more clearly now and accepted that the differences between us were smaller than the things we held in common. Maybe it was just a survival thing taking over at last. We realised we needed each other;

needed Jack's constant moving on; needed Danny's practical skills and knowledge of the terrain and needed Josh, because... because he had become a part of us which we couldn't leave behind.

\*

Days and weeks went by. We lost count. Anyway there didn't seem much point trying to keep track of time. Time is only needed when you have to meet someone, some place when you need to be in 'sync' with other people. The only people around was the bunch of us walking together – joined at the hip.

We managed to zig-zag our way between small villages finding a few scraps to eat and drink in local stores. When we ran out of bottled water we would catch rainwater in the fold of our waterproofs and feed the precious liquid into an empty plastic bottle. we shared the water we had. After losing Jenny we seemed to look after each other more.

It rained most days with raindrops like bullets exploding in the pools on the track and seeping, cold into our boots and socks. the earth was sodden, like a sponge unable to soak up any more – rejecting the source of life. For every soul that once inhabited this place there were a thousand, million drops of rain now. The sky seemed to be intent on washing the earth clean, to rid it of all traces of man.

\*

We set off again heading west. The snow was melting fast.

After a few hours we were on higher ground where the floodwaters hadn't reached. At the edge of one of the fields, near a swollen brook, was the strange sight of a railway carriage, stranded like some great fish out of water. That was when we saw the other two, sat outside the carriage tending the beginnings of a fire.

One of them offered us coffee and we were glad of the warmth. We were happy to share our fire but somehow I felt uncomfortable even from the word go. One of them got to talking with Josh and Jack, talking about what would happen with society breaking down and there being no-one to keep law and order: "What is there to keep people civilised?" he asked. "Why would folks stick together and live by any rules? Why would we even respect the life of others?"

Jack and Josh both had things to say about human nature and behaviour, which might give you a kind of hope for the future. I don't know how much they really believed what they said, but it was kind of reassuring that two guys like them could say those things. Jack said he was very clear that people would seek each other out in all this mess and some kind of groupings or societies would reform where people could rely on some basic rules of life and could share the task of building homes and growing food.

Jack said he thought it was just human nature that people would do that. He said we have a fundamental need for our fellow man and we would find it impossible to continue for long alone. He even said that if we couldn't find others we would have to invent them like as if we were mad, because without them we couldn't even be sure we existed ourselves.

Josh said people were basically selfish but that very selfishness would bring them together as we needed other people to survive.

The men from the railway carriage didn't seem so sure. It seemed like they had had some arguments about this or something else. Any way they didn't seem to like each other much and I began to wonder why these two were together.

"What do you do if there's not enough food or fresh water to go around?" asked one of them. "If there's two of you, and rations only for one, then someone is going to go without. What one eats and drinks another doesn't. How do you think people will react? I can tell you brotherly love will be in short supply. For instance, you have your rucksack and I'm betting you have some food and water in there to keep you going until the next scavenging opportunity. How would it be if I just took them now? I don't suppose you'd just sit tight and say help yourself would you? Not unless your cowardice was bigger than your hunger, unless one kind of fear was bigger than another."

I remember feeling really uncomfortable as he spoke and the hairs on the back of my neck were standing up. I felt really confused like *myself* was slipping away through my fingers and I couldn't catch me no matter how hard I tried.

It was then he got out the knife. I can't remember much of what happened after that.

*

We stood at the base of a hill and looked up towards a farmhouse and outbuildings. Our feet crunched on the gravel track as we drew nearer to one of the large barns. Outside, hens were running around a pen and stabbing their beaks at the dirt. In the field to the left was a horse grazing and beyond a dozen or more sheep.

Jack approached the barn door cautiously and took hold of the large, rusting, iron bolt and slid it across with one hand whilst pulling on the great door with the other. The hinges screamed in protest as it opened. The smell of straw filled our nostrils. After a few moments hesitation we stumbled into the semi-darkness.

It took some time for our eyes to get used to the dark. Gradually stables to the left and a huge stack of bales to the right formed out of the gloom. In front was a pile of sugar beet and some upended wheelbarrows. "Looks like the roof's in good nick. It's dry in here. We could kip down for the night," Josh said. "Those hens looked plump; I'm sure Danny can show us how to prepare one for a roast."

Suddenly a voice came from behind us: "Who are you; what are you doing here? This is private land." We turned to see a tall, wiry man with his arms folded, cradling a shotgun.

"Whoa, we don't mean any harm," Jack replied. Been travelling and saw the farmstead from the valley below. Didn't know there was anybody living here." Jack held out his hand and started to walk towards the man.

"That's far enough," said the man lifting the stock of the shotgun.

"Haven't seen anybody on the road for days now. Met a couple some time back but... they stayed on where we met. Been looking for food and water; don't want any trouble. Is this your place? Just a bite to eat and some fresh water and we'll be on our way if you're not taking anyone in. A dry night's sleep would be welcome though."

The man let the shotgun barrel fall half way and with the stock braced under one arm he waved towards the door, saying: "Come with me."

# EPILOGUE

"Well, what do you think?"

"I'm not sure. He seems to have been travelling for a long time. There are a lot of gaps. I need to ask him a few questions before I can make a proper assessment."

"Be my guest. We haven't been able to get much out of him so far."

"What's your name?" The man directed his question at the figure slumped in the chair in front of him. "We can't help you if you're not willing to communicate with us; nobody here is going to harm you. It's just that… well… we are a small group here and we have to be careful about taking any others in."

"How have you kept going all this time; where did you find food and clean water?"

The figure sat silent, head down, breathing shallowly.

"See what I mean. He clammed up and has been like that since just after we found him. Just mumbling every now and again that's all."

"Mumbling what?"

"Too indistinct to make out."

"I'm intrigued by the others he was travelling with and the relationship between them all. The writer of the journal seems to have gotten an intimate knowledge of each of them; seems like they told him a lot and yet…"

"What?"

"The writer doesn't have much to say about his own feelings; about how all this mess affected him. He doesn't have much to do with the others either, you know, interacting with them. It's like he was watching and listening to them without really engaging himself."

"So what do you make of that?"

Well, it's…"

"Danny," the hooded figure shrugged his shoulders and mumbled.

The two men fell quiet as if trying to leave space for the mystery to continue to unravel.

"Danny. Your name is Danny; is that right?"

The figure remained still, with no reply.

"Where are you from Danny? My name is Peter and this here is Joe. We want to help you Danny if we can. You're safe here. Whatever happened, you are safe here now."

Silence. The two men looked at each other.

"Maybe we better just leave him for a while," said Joe. "Eventually he's going to get hungry; that should loosen his tongue. I'd like to help the guy out but we've got limited resources here. We can't take on any passengers and if he's going to continue behaving like this he's going to be a liability, a dead weight."

Joe turned in the direction of the door.

"Maldon," said the figure, more clearly this time. "I'm Danny. I'm not afraid."

"'Bout time," said Joe.

"Well, Danny from Maldon, would you like to tell us how you got here. We've read the journal you were carrying but it seems to run out. It must have taken a few days to get here, during which time you parted company with the other two guys; Jack and Josh – those were their names weren't they? Or, I suppose there were three others; the other being whoever wrote this journal. I don't think that was you Danny was it?"

"Didn't write nothing. Can't," Danny said.

"Can you remember what happened, Danny?" asked Peter.

Again the figure fell silent.

"Where are Jack and Josh?" Peter continued.

"Who?"

"Come on, the other two guys in here, the guys you were with; where did they go?" Joe pressed in frustration.

"Don't know. Don't know them," came the response.

"Listen, mate, if you're going to carry on like this then I suggest you leave the farm here and make your own way; we don't have space for time wasters here…" Joe's voice sharpened.

"I don't think bullying him is going to work," said Peter.

"We're assuming that the contents of the journal are factual, really happened," Peter continued. "It may just be a story, fiction. But then who's the author if it's not Danny here? I'm not sure what to make of it."

"Where did you get this from, Danny?" Peter pointed at the journal laying open on the table between them.

"Mine," Danny said.

"It's yours; OK but if you didn't write it, Danny, who did? And are your friends Josh and Jack real or just the figment of some author's imagination?"

"He wrote it," Danny responded.

"Who?"

"The other."

"Jesus," snapped Joe, "we aren't getting anywhere here."

"Wait. Who is this 'other', Danny?" probed Peter.

"Dunno. He just comes and goes like."

"Has this 'other' got a name?"

"Dunno."

"Where is he now, Danny?" Peter asked.

"He left. I don't know where he is. Left days ago, a week, mebbee more."

The three fell silent again.

"How long have you been travelling, Danny?" Peter decided to try a different tack.

Danny looked up and stared at Peter with empty eyes. He paused for a few moments then said: "A week, maybe more."

"Either this guy's lost his marbles or he's taking the piss," snorted Joe.

"Where did it start, Danny?" Peter persisted.

"The big flood, big wave. Washed us away. Woke up not sure where; didn't recognise much to start with." The words were coming more freely now.

"Then what?" asked Peter.

"Mum. Needed to look for Mum. I started walkin'. There was bodies, lots of bodies."

"Were you in London, Danny?"

"Got out. Got out before it hit. Walkin' east. Needed to head back home."

"Is that when you met Jack and Josh?" Peter prompted.

"Who are they?"

"So what happened then?"

"I followed the railway tracks to stay out of the water. Just kept walkin'. Town was deserted but there was some food in the supermarket. I stayed there for some nights but then I needed to get on and look for Mum, so I left."

Joe looked at Peter.

"The poor sod's been wanderin' around for over a

year since the evacuation of London. Christ knows why he hasn't been picked up before or how he's kept body and soul together. Maybe he hasn't. His head's pretty messed up if you ask me."

"He's been looking for his mother," Peter responded.

"My guess is he's been going round and round in circles in the flooded areas of East Essex. At least, I think that's where the journal points. The authorities declared that a no-go area just a few days after the surge hit; no way we were going to be able to reclaim and rehabilitate that land. People were left to fend for themselves, those few who survived."

Danny was listening intently, his head now swivelled sideways inside the hood of his jacket.

Not until that moment had Peter caught sight of the livid wound on the side of Danny's face, still weeping.

"Where did you get that from, Danny? You need something on that otherwise it looks set to turn septic lad. We'll see what we've got in the first aid supplies. How did it happen?"

Danny raised his hand gingerly to his face and felt the ragged edge of the wound.

"Must've hit it on a tree branch or something," he mumbled.

Joe shot a sceptical glance at Peter.

"So when you left town, where did you head," Joe continued the questioning.

"I don't rightly know. Just kept walkin'. Fell in the water, I think but dragged myself out. There was some shootin' one time."

"Did you see anybody else, Danny?"

"Don't recall. Maybe. My mum; she was with a man making a campfire. She was nice to me. We stayed there for a while until ..."

"Until what?"

"She fell off the bridge; went into the river. We couldn't find her. No! Hold on! Mum!"

Danny's head fell.

Minutes passed in silence. Joe shifted his weight from one foot to another, then back again.

Suddenly the hooded figure started to mumble at first quietly in a whisper; then gradually as the volume turned up, a different voice, a polished, public school accent emerged from under the hood: "I told Jack we needed to stay away. But he insisted didn't he? The man never listens; what qualifies him to act like he's in charge all the time? Unelected leader. It's his kind that got us into this mess. When is he going to get it; things have changed; the old order has gone."

"Christ!" whispered Joe. "This guy's weird. This is creepy. Let's get him out of here. We've got enough of our own troubles without dealing with this."

The hooded figure continued: "It's always the same. As soon as we have anything to do with others, we get let down some way. Better off on our own; better off under those arches with our own fire to keep warm by. People stink; always after what's good for them…"

"He's switching," said Peter.

"What?"

"He is taking on another personality."

"I don't understand."

"Well I can't be sure. It's a long time since I covered this in the clinical psychology class but there is a condition called 'Dissociative Identity Disorder,' Peter whispered.

"… Jack's just the same. He'll ditch us as soon as he's found somewhere he feels safe. Somewhere else he can be in charge without the need for the rest of us…"

"What's that?" Joe demanded.

"You might call it split personality," replied Peter. "It's a psychiatric disorder characterised by having one or more 'alter' personalities that control behaviour."

"You mean this guy really is crazy?"

"You can use that term if you want but this is a very specific form of mental illness."

The hooded man continued talking in the background. Peter went on: "There's no unifying consciousness or 'self' like you and I. This guy is at least two, probably more, personalities in one body, each 'alter' appearing spontaneously without him having any conscious control over when they appear. In fact to talk of 'him' is misleading. There is no one central character or personality. Consciousness and memory is, sort of, divided up amongst the different 'alters'. Each one can have a distinct personal history, self-image or identity including a separate name. The characteristics of the 'alters' are often very different from each other. There may be many of them."

"Jack's one of the guys in the journal. I never thought…"

"Me neither. But the memory gaps were an indicator. The condition carries an inability to recall important personal information, more than just ordinary forgetfulness. Big swathes of the person's history just go missing. I realise now that was one of the things that made the journal so odd; the way it described parts of Josh, Jack and Danny's histories but left big gaps."

"And he couldn't remember where he'd been for the last week or so," Joe filled in.

"So who's talking now?"

"Think back to the journal. It sounds like the way I imagined Josh; that resentful voice criticising Jack," replied Peter.

"How did he get like this?"

"I can only speculate. There is general agreement that the cause is repressed memories of childhood abuse. Sufferers redraw their boundaries as a kind of protection mechanism. The abuse is so horrific and painful to contemplate that the victim sort of 'leaves', erects a boundary so that the horror can't happen to them, rather to some other self.

"The underlying dissociation can manifest itself later in adult life after the initial childhood trauma. It can be triggered by situations of overwhelming stress. The floods and dislocation could have brought it on; maybe the fears over what happened to Danny's, 'their', mother or maybe some other incident on the journey here. We may never know what sparked it but the roots of the disorder lie much further back in childhood."

"In a sense it's a kind of defence mechanism. When faced with an overwhelmingly traumatic situation from which there is no escape the individual just 'goes away' in their head. It's a defence against acute physical or emotional pain or anxious anticipation of such pain. By dissociating the thoughts, feelings and memories of the traumatic experience it can be separated off psychologically, allowing the person to function as if the trauma had not happened.

"Wait. In the journal Danny got cut in the face in a fight with Josh. See, the wound, still there. How could that have happened unless Josh was real?"

"In some sense Josh is 'real', at least as 'real' as Danny. But self-mutilation is another associated feature of this disorder," Peter explained.

The hooded figure had fallen quiet again.

"So the poor sod was subject to abuse when he was younger. I remember the journal said his father had left the family when Danny was a teenager; do you think that was connected?"

"Maybe. But which history is the real one? Josh was in conflict with an authoritarian father and Jack came from a broken marriage. Which family history is real or are they all slices of the truth? Anyway it doesn't have to have been a family member that was a source of the abuse, although I can understand your assumption."

Josh had been quiet for a few moments when suddenly a strong Northern accent erupted from the huddled figure.

"I'm sick and tired of your snivelling. All along you've complained and been negative at every turn. Why don't you just push off and leave; see how long you survive out there by yourself. We'll travel a lot quicker without you dragging your heels and whingeing all the time. Just piss off…"

"The 'alters' are often not only very different characters but are in overt conflict with each other," Peter continued. "Switching between them is often brought on by stressful situations."

"So they know each other exists, these 'alters'?" asked Joe.

"You can hear two of them in dialogue now. It's clear from the journal that the three Jack, Josh and Danny recognised each other, although there was some 'disappearing' happening. It seems they each knew the 'narrator' as well because they told him, or her, some of their histories and what they were thinking; they seem to have confided in him or her. This can happen particularly when the individual is in the earlier stages of, or recovering from, the disorder."

"What do you mean 'disappearing'?"

"One of the characters kind of falls off the edge of the stage; doesn't seem to be in the scene and isn't engaged with the others."

"Happens to a lot of people doesn't it?"

"Not like this; the one disappearing pops out of existence. Did you notice in the journal the narrator wasn't present for everything that went on between the three; there were discontinuities, gaps in the journal's description of the journey? When Jack went off with the rations the narrator went with him and it took time for the others to reappear when Jack returned to the camp."

"So what's happening?"

"One or more of the 'alters' takes control and dominates so much that other alters are squeezed out; they kind of get pushed through the cracks in time and when they return they have a sense of having lost time which they can't account for."

"How can they have different histories if they are

really just different faces of the same individual?"

"They don't; well not in our sense. Each personality experiences life as if it had its own distinct personal history and identity. We don't know what the 'alters' represent or what determines the identities they manifest. But it's possible that they are a mixture of repressed sub-personalities or possible life courses that the primary identity never realised.

"Anyway, I think in some way each 'alter' must serve a purpose, have some role."

"What do you mean?"

"Well, Josh and Jack often seemed to be in conflict. But they kept going through the hardships. It seems like they spurred each other on or gave the other some *raison d'etre*, some reason to carry on, if only to 'show' the other. Danny had a role in the journey too, as conciliator. When he threatened to leave the other two calmed down; it was as if they recognised they needed him, had to keep him with them."

"So they kind of need each other; can't live together but can't live apart?"

"Yes."

"So what's going to happen to this guy, these guys, now?"

"It's not clear whether he is in the early stages of the disorder or whether he is in the recovery phase. The last parts of the journal suggest some reconciliation was underway between the three personalities. Josh and Jack were taking care of Danny and there was less friction between them.

"This acceptance of each other is essential to recovery. A process of integration or synthesis is needed for full recovery where a core identity starts to crystallise and communicates with each of the alters accepting them as parts of a whole. Usually long-term therapy is needed to treat the disorder by facilitating this mutual awareness between the alters and by addressing the underlying emotional issues of each personality which stemmed from the original trauma."

"So you think he's maybe on the road to recovery? But listen to him just now Jack and Josh are still fighting with each other."

"Yes. It's a progressive thing, whether the disorder is starting or the patient is in recovery. You'll get backsliding even in recovery. But it's just as possible he is in the early stages. These floods and the deprivation that's come with them could be the trigger that's brought the disorder to the surface."

"I still don't get how there is no single, central

personality. Surely there was, if you go right back to whoever it was that suffered the 'trauma' as you put it; before he split into different parts. Was that Jack or Josh or Danny? Where did it start?"

"It could have been any of them or none of them. They seem evenly balanced in the journal. It's not as if one of them is really dominant."

"You say it might have been none of the three?"

"We may not have heard the voice of the 'host', the core identity; we may not even have heard all of the alters. Sometimes alters are dormant, in the background and it requires a specific trigger to evoke them."

"What about the narrator?"

"Yes. We know almost nothing about the narrator. He, or maybe it's a she, is just an observer of events."

"Could the narrator be the core identity or 'host'?"

"It's possible."

"Strange."

"What is?"

"Well, maybe we all have a touch of this disorder. Don't you think?" Joe asked.

"Go on."

"Well, isn't it just a question of degree? Ok, I don't have a bunch of guys who seem to have completely different histories and speak with different accents. But still I think I am more than one personality. It's like a different guy comes out sometimes; you should see me behind the wheel of a car…!"

The huddled figure began to speak again: "It's almost impossible to be alone. Even when there is no one else in the room there are at least two people in my head. There's the one who keeps noticing things; the one who just can't help chattering on, like he's singing in the dark to keep something at bay. He just can't keep quiet or he can't bear the quiet. Then there's another one who seems like he is quietness itself. He says nothing and he can only be glimpsed out of the corner of your eye when nothing else is happening, when there's nothing else going on to divert your attention. He seems like he might be the real me, the heart of me but he's like impossible to know; he never shows himself, steps out into the open so you can see what he looks like. Maybe if I could stop the chattering then I'd see this other guy more clearly, more head on."

"It's a different voice this time," said Joe.

"Are you the one who kept the journal?" Peter

asked the hooded figure.

The figure stopped rocking.

"Are you the one who wrote this?" Peter waved the journal in the air.

"I think he was talking as the narrator just now, and referring to one or more alters. What is your name?"

"No name. I am no name."

"What are you doing here?"

"I came with the others, until…"

"Until what?"

"There was a fight. We had knives."

"Who was fighting?"

"They wouldn't do as I said, always wanting to do something different. Just full of shit all of them. Know it alls. I hate them; hate them. I couldn't put up with anymore; listening to all their stuff as if they were the only ones who mattered, the only ones who had any pain. What right did they have to say what should happen? Who did they think they were anyway? We were running out of food and water and all they could do was argue. Sometimes they'd pretend to get on, pretend they would look after each other but I knew, I knew what kind of people they were. Just interested in their selves, nobody else. They were bad, rotten. Deserved it."

"Deserved what?"

The figure started rocking again. This time emitting a high-pitched whine.

At that moment another man pushed through the door, breathless.

"Peter... Peter there's something down at the brook you should see," he said, white faced.

"What is it? We just need to finish with this guy."

"You need to come now..."

Peter reluctantly followed, leaving Joe to continue, uneasily, quizzing the mystery intruder.

A few hundred yards from the farmstead, beyond the gravel path, ran a swollen brook, gouging a wound through the fields. The rain was lashing down again, driven by the wind, stinging the men's faces red. Morning storm waters were running brown in rivulets off the saturated fields, stripping away turf and topsoil.

They headed towards a small stand of Alders and Willows, hanging onto mother earth with their branches windmilling, whirling furiously as the storm stripped the last of their autumn leaves. The limbs of the trees moaned as they bent with the Easterly wind.

The two men clung onto the rims of their caps,

peering out from underneath the tweed as they approached the trees, half closing their watery eyes against the storm.

Then suddenly lightning cracked the sky allowing them to make sense of the dark bundles on the ground ahead.

As they pushed against the gale force wind, the bundles resolved into two, no, three bodies sprawling, lifeless, in the damp earth under the trees.

"Christ! Who are these guys? Have you called the police?"

"Just now. They're on their way."

One of the figures was dressed in a businessman's pin-striped suit with red braces and tie; another a giant of a man, his hands clutching the soil as if trying to hold onto life; the third, with a heavy black, matted hair and beard, his face frozen in a sardonic smile.

## THE END

# ABOUT THE AUTHOR

Born in West Yorkshire, Stephen has an Honours degree in Mathematics and Philosophy. He is married and has two boys. After three years school teaching in London, he joined a City firm where he became a partner. Parenting, philosophy and his career have taught him to look at life through questioning eyes and to expect the unexpected.

This is the second of two adult novels written by Stephen. His earlier work, Anselm's Gift, is a coming-of-age story.

Printed in Great Britain
by Amazon